IN
THE
BEGINNING

IN
THE
BEGINNING

The Origin of Koreans

PEJAY BRADLEY

Cover and interior design by Tabitha Lahr
Cover and interior images © Shutterstock.com

Published 2025
Printed in the United States of America
ISBN: 978-1-7336057-3-1
E-ISBN: 978-1-7336057-4-8
Library of Congress Control Number: 2025902355

For information, email: pjkimb@gmail.com

To my grandchildren,
Elodie, Gordon, and Charlie

CHAPTER 1

I n the beginning, it all started. This was around five thousand years ago, or so was I taught at an early age—maybe when I was seven.

As I approached the end of my being, the end of my vibrant life, I began to dream of a personal visit to that era. My longing for it grew dense, thick, and monolithic. I fell into an unwavering obsession with wandering around the land of the primeval era, feeling the air of five thousand years ago, when my DNA started. A search for the truth; a search for the origin of my being, most of all. I was the center of my universe, and knowing the beginning of myself was all that mattered to me. It was always *I* that was relevant, to the point that I could be labeled narcissistic or even egocentric. But who would not be so, in truth?

I made up my mind to explore the ancient world, whatever it might take to do so. Once I stated this intention, I was relieved of the anxiety that had consumed me for the past months—or, more accurately, years. This anxiety had arisen from my hesitation, misdirection, helplessness, and hopelessness. As soon as I found a potential solution, no matter how flimsy and even wild it might be, the pulse of ecstasy flowed through my veins. I saw myself strolling through virgin forests, experiencing clouds, winds, and sun rays of long ago, breathing in the fresh fragrance of unspoiled earth. I saw myself witnessing a hole opening in the sky to spew out three thousand men and women toward the Earth with a young deity named Whan-Woong to lead them; I saw myself as a bear turning into a young woman in a cave; I saw myself, as this bear lady, wedding the ruler from Heaven; I saw myself, as her, giving birth to our first king, who ruled the vast territory of the northeastern Asian continent in the beginning.

The box I was looking for was within easy reach. It was the brown, varnished wooden one, shoved into a corner of my home office, into which I threw business cards handed to me by strangers and acquaintances alike.

Rooting through hundreds of cards, I was lucky to find the one I wanted within minutes. On a plain white background, *Willard McGordon, PhD, Department of Science Engineering, Stamperd University* was embossed in an elegant font, followed by telephone numbers and an email address. Delighted, I also soon found myself paralyzed by indecision. *What do I do?* I wondered. *Should I text, call, or email him? Will he see me, or remember me? Will he even respond to my message?*

In this uncertain state, I let a few wasted days go by before finally bringing myself to the seat before my laptop at the breakfast table, the sunniest spot in my little house, and starting to tap the keyboard.

> *Dear Professor McGordon, I hope you'll find a few minutes to see me at your earliest convenience. We met about three years ago at an award ceremony for Jay Henry Kim on campus. I do not expect you to remember me, but I have a serious matter I would like to see you about. My best contact for your reply would be this email address.*
> *Sincerely, Peonia Kim*

"The world is full of surprises," I marveled to myself when I received his reply a week later. *I can see you, Peonia, between 3 and 4 on Friday afternoon next week at my office. Let me know if that suits you.*

My heart pounded in response to the offer. The chance of receiving such an answer had felt remote, and yet it had come to me like an apple falling into my bag as I passed a tree on the street. He had even called me by my first name.

Stamperd University was the world's leader in physics and engineering science. Professor McGordon's name, meanwhile, had rotated in and out of the reputable science magazines for over a decade as they reported on his progress in inventing something revolutionary: a time machine. As controversial as the machine was, McGordon had drawn wild attention for several years while his project was in its nascent stages, but he had since faded into oblivion. Perhaps it had become obvious to the public, after those first years, that the prospect of actually traveling into the past or future was still far from realization.

I didn't yet know for a fact that Professor McGordon had succeeded in his efforts, but my instincts told me he had built his time machine, had it fully operational, and was searching for an initial rider, someone who would be undaunted by the challenge and unconditionally committed.

All the puzzle pieces were falling into the right places; I was sure of it.

At three o'clock on the designated Friday, I pulled my car into the Stamperd guest parking lot at the end of immaculate flower gardens surrounded by smooth green lawns. Situated in the greater San Francisco Bay Area, the school enjoyed a backdrop of mountains, forests, and the Pacific Ocean over and beyond the hilly terrain.

I had been on the campus a few times in recent years and remembered the hostile parking situation more clearly than the beauty of the campus. Indeed, on this day every parking space in the lot seemed to be taken, and I panicked. I did not want to be late to this first meeting of such enormous importance.

I finally found a spot at the end of a row and pulled my car in, triumphantly reciting my favorite phrase, "There is always one for me."

Professor McGordon's office was located on the ground floor in the farthest corner of his building from the front gate. A few minutes after I nervously knocked on his door, he opened it to let out a young man, perhaps a student, and let me in.

He offered me a seat across the desk from his own, a stuffy leather chair from a bygone era. The office was cluttered with books, magazines, unrecognizable devices, and even more bizarre gadgets; the air was stale with the odor of old books. I carefully settled into the leather seat, tense with the understanding of just how crucial this meeting was for me. I had prepared impressive words for the occasion but forgot every one of them now, at my moment of need.

Professor McGordon, meanwhile, showed no feelings even remotely resembling mine. He seemed indifferent to my anxiety and unaware of my motive for the visit. He looked mostly the way I remembered him—clean-shaven, ruddy complexion, blue eyes— although his golden waves on top now had some salt sprinkles. He wore what I took to be his usual, a dark gray vest over a white oxford shirt, no tie.

"You have a nice office." Realizing what a cliché this was, I rushed to recover from the trite remark. "I mean, it's very becoming a scientist's office." In fact, I did not know how a scientist's office should look, and this latter remark sounded even worse.

"Good to see you, Peonia," he said, not seeming to notice my awkwardness. "How is Henry doing?"

Jay Henry Kim was my nephew, through whom I had met Professor McGordon twice. Henry did his post-doctoral program under McGordon, and the professor once proclaimed that he had never before known a student as bright and promising as Henry. McGordon offered Henry a position on his research team, but Henry had politely declined and instead accepted a position in a reputable university in his hometown—Seoul, Korea.

It was good to know why and how the professor remembered me, but I had no intention of wasting my time with him talking about my nephew, no matter how beloved he was to me. I wanted to get on with this conversation. "He's fine," I said. "But would you like to know why I've come to see you, Professor?"

"Of course," he responded in a dry tone.

"Thank you." I paused, thinking he might venture a guess, but he just sat there. Unable to bear the silence for even a few seconds longer, I started to babble: "I'm a liberal arts person, and I'll be the last one to understand the mechanism of a time machine . . ."

At the sound of the phrase "time machine," Professor

McGordon showed a slight agitation, but he quickly regained his composure. For a moment, I imagined I heard him shouting, "You, too, scoundrel! Snooping on my baby!" But he maintained a placid expression.

"I'd very much like to know about it, to see it, to touch it, and even to . . ."

Before I let the word "ride" escape my lips, I paused again, waiting for his reaction. His silence felt like a loud and clear "Leave!" He seemed determined to remain quiet and ignore me. A part of me, crushed, thought it would be best to leave him then, but I nonetheless felt compelled to air out my deepest feelings, or at least a portion of them, before I departed.

". . . even to experiment with a short ride," I said. "What would it take to do so?" Surprised by my own audacity and persistence, I continued more confidently, "I'm firmly committed and will handle any and all difficulties, and I'll pay you whatever cost you demand for a ride."

He remained unmoved, not even looking at me. It was clearly time for me to leave. Lingering there for even one more second would only annoy him, I thought, so I left the room without attempting any of the usual parting rituals.

Professor McGordon's reaction to my request was not unexpected, so I was not particularly offended by it. Rather, I hoped I had not offended or disappointed him.

It's only the beginning, I told myself. I had made myself clear, and in that sense, accomplished my mission.

I walked toward the parking lot feeling better than I had in months.

CHAPTER 2

A week later, I received an email from Professor McGordon that read simply, *Would you like to continue our discussion?*

I nearly fell off my chair. I wondered if I had read the message correctly. *Was this a dream, or a joke?*

It seemed impossible that it was otherwise, but I nevertheless wasted no time in replying to him. *Certainly. Let me know when and where.*

This time, I had to be more specific, precise, and convincing regarding what I had in mind. So, the night before our meeting, I stayed up late, staring at the ceiling in the dark, crafting a speech that would communicate all I wanted to convey to him—and do so in style.

We'd agreed to meet at a Starbucks not far from campus. We walked in at the same time from opposite directions.

"I am glad to see you again," I said calmly, suppressing my excitement.

"Let's get something to drink," Professor McGordon responded with a nod.

"Yes, of course."

We settled in tall chairs in a corner of the café and exchanged faint smiles. I waited a minute for him to initiate conversation.

When I realized no overture was coming from him, I opened. "You see, my heritage speaks to me louder and louder these days."

"What do you mean?" he asked.

"Well, more precisely, I suppose my conscience is the voice that speaks to me lately." I took a sip of my iced latte. "I have read so many stories from the past—Greek mythologies, Roman legends, Jewish history, the Arabian Nights, Norse myths, German folklore . . . And there are many more of these sorts of texts out in the world: national origin stories, histories mixed with myths and legends. Yet I know of not one single Korean legend that's available to global readers. I feel it's my mission to deliver one of those stories to the world." I thought I sounded better than I had when we'd spoken in his office; I was succeeding in making it clear that this was a mission, something greater than a mere personal DNA search.

"That's marvelous, but I'm not a writer. I'm afraid I'm not even a reader of anything except articles related to my field." The professor sipped his black coffee. "I was forced to read those mythologies during my college days, of course; a few grabbed my interest, but none have survived in my memory."

"How interesting," I said. "I mean, how different people are."

I tried to explain that my interest was pinned to what had happened five thousand years earlier in the land of Korea, which was then the peninsula plus Manchuria. I told him that I longed for a visit to the era in which my country, my people, and myself had originated. "An era when the world was filled with the swooshing sounds of the wind, rolling leaves on the ground, and pure air," I told him. "When wild animals romped around freely and happily, all living together in peace and harmony, as the edible berries and fruits were sufficiently abundant then to feed all lives on Earth. I know you can help me with that journey."

Professor McGordon dropped his eyes into his coffee cup as if in deep contemplation.

"I firmly believe the trip will be worth all the cost and risk," I said, leaning forward in my seat. "Legends may be grounded in fact or imagination, and there are always reasons why they are the way they are. In our ancient era, legends rich with facts took shape, and today those marvels have been uncovered only partially. No one has presented them in whole to the world yet.

They deserve to be explored, exposed, evaluated, and enjoyed. I am taking that task upon myself as my mission. You must help, or you will be committing a great disservice to"—I scrambled for the right words—"uh . . . to the world, to the truth, and to our intelligence. I believe I have enough to pay for my share of the cost of the trip, and even to defray the past costs you have incurred building the machine."

"Not unexpected." Saying this, the professor lifted his eyes from the coffee cup and managed a slight smile, looking directly into my eyes. I knew he was not the type to show emotion. This indistinct smile from him felt as meaningful as a hearty laugh would have from many others.

Appearing to be in a better mood now than when he had arrived, the professor began to throw out a few personal questions—when had I come to this country, where had I gone to school, what I was doing for a living, and so on. After a short pause, he even asked if I had a family. I responded casually. I wanted to return all those friendly questions, but I held myself back from doing so because it seemed more important to stay on track.

I sensed that the professor was evading any direct mention of the time machine, circumventing the very subject I had come to talk with him about. This was not completely unexpected, however, and I did not want to rush or force him into it. I resigned myself to giving him time to dance around the true subject matter at hand.

We parted for the second time with no visible gains for me. I wasn't bothered by this, though, because

I sensed that I was in fact getting closer to where I wanted to go.

Later that day, he emailed me. *Did I ask too many personal questions of you? I think I did, and I apologize.*

Hardly! I replied without delay.

Little by little, he seemed to become more receptive to my wish to learn about his time machine. At our fourth meeting, he finally admitted that he was in possession of it. He explained that he had hidden it from the public eye for a reason. He did not want the publicity when its functions were yet to be proven; he wanted to introduce the machine to the public only after a successful operation. He was, in fact, secretly looking for a volunteer.

Importantly, he also wanted strong justification for the machine's use. What would he achieve by operating it? Trips to the future could potentially cause enormous chaos and turmoil; trips to the past, he thought, might be futile and irrelevant, not worth the trouble of operating the machine.

Over time, I convinced him that my proposed trip to the past would be worthwhile.

Or perhaps he convinced himself.

Before we hammered out the details of my mission, I offered a name for the machine.

"How about we call it 'Ray'?" I suggested.

"Ray?"

"Yes," I said, "because it's a ray—a ray of hope, a ray of guidance, and a ray of fulfilment to me."

"Hm . . ." He tapped his chin. "I never thought of naming it before, but yes, I like it."

"Wonderful!" I clapped my hands together. "It can also serve as a code between us."

It was at this point that he began to instruct me on how to control and operate Ray—how to turn it on and off, set the time of visit, steer into the right course in space, and land at the correct site. All of these steps had to be accurately programmed at the start of the ride; the entire flight would then automatically follow the programmed instructions.

"I will help you at the time of your departure," he said, "but you must remember it all for the return trip." He further explained that he did not want to leave any trace of my journey in his computer, and I must carefully note every detail for my own sake.

At the end of his instructions, I reiterated my offer to contribute funds to help defray the cost of building Ray to begin with.

"I appreciate your offer, and I will take you up on it," he said, nodding. "I just have to come up with some final figures."

Having cleared all the details, we agreed that I would ride Ray in a month. The final preparations for the trip required calculating the year and choosing a landing spot. He agreed to my proposal of the year 2372 BC at Baekdu Mountain, which sits between Manchuria and the Korean peninsula.

I closed my eyes for a moment, already feeling and smelling the ancient world I was headed toward. All seemed so unreal yet so real, so far yet so near, so wild yet so controlled. I pinched my own arm.

This was really happening.

My phone rang as I was packing a small suitcase for my trip.

"Peonia," Professor McGordon said, "I've decided to go with you."

"Umm . . ." I stammered as my heart jumped high and fast. I swallowed my initial gasp and managed to utter, "Lovely!" followed by a nervous, "What did you say?"

How I had wished, all this time, that he would accompany me—but after his initial declaration that I was on my own, I had believed it was an impossibility. I had accepted a solo flight, but I was not and never would be ready for it. I suspect a part of me hadn't given up hope that he would change his mind. Now, I had my wish: he would be riding by my side.

"I thought it over," he said, "and I realized you could use my help in operating Ray."

"I can't tell you how relieved I am." I let out a deep sigh, my heart still rapidly throbbing.

"I see." He cleared his throat. "It's settled, then. But we must reschedule the departure for a later date."

"It's your call now," I said quickly. "Just tell me when."

"I won't make you wait too long. How about an additional month or so?"

"That's better for me, to tell you the truth." I felt out of breath. With my meager, clumsy mechanical talent, I had been terrified that my journey would end up being a one-way trip. Now I would certainly have a round-trip ticket.

And I wanted to come back.

CHAPTER 3

It was a sunny day, as usual, in California.

In the previous week, I had ensured that my utilities would be turned off while I was away, scheduled automatic payments for all my bills, and informed my neighbors that I would be travelling for up to a couple years, without telling them where I was going.

Before I left that late August afternoon, I secured all my doors and windows.

I walked out of my house with one bag filled with dresses, blouses, pants, skirts, sandals, sneakers, and heavy coats, all simply designed, plus a blanket, toiletries, a sewing kit, and saltine crackers. I deliberately left out all the modern gadgets, like a cell phone, a camera, a recording device, or even writing pads, pens, pencils, and many others. No one in that era had even imagined such items, and I was ready to endure a primitive life with them. Most of all, I trusted my memory and knew all I experienced would be safely stored in my memory tank.

Uber took me to the address Professor McGordon had given me: an old, Victorian-style house in a quiet neighborhood. It was around 5:00 p.m., the hour we'd chosen together.

The professor greeted me at the door. I did not see anyone else inside or outside the house and wondered whether he had a family. But I was determined not to violate the rule I had set for myself against poking into his private life.

He first led me to the backyard, where a shed stood detached from his house. It appeared recently built, but not by a professional. It had clearly been constructed by a layman—likely the professor himself. He opened the small door on the side of the redwood structure.

As we walked in, the stuffy air greeted me first; then I was confronted by an unfamiliar object snugly fit into the space.

"Is this it?" I asked, eyes wide.

"Yes," he said, "this is it."

The shed's front door looked like a regular garage door bolted from the inside. All of the windowless walls were tightly paneled in redwood except for the metal door we had just entered through. The roof was covered with plexiglass panels, and a rolled-up tarp was visible at the rear end of the ceiling. But what arrested my attention was the thing sitting in the center of the room: an object I had dreamed of for years and many scientists had long sought after.

My heart pumped faster as I studied the dark shape. It was Ray, the time machine, there before my eyes, looking a bit like an oddly designed car. The top part was a dome studded with tiny solar panels. The front hood was short, the back line dropped steeply, and its four wheels were much smaller than car tires. The entire machine was a deep gray, most inconspicuous, which he might have chosen to deter unwanted attention. What most surprised me was that the machine lacked intricate complexity in its design, as far as I could tell. The complex part of the mechanism, I decided, must be under the hood.

The professor took my luggage from my hand, moved around Ray with ease, opened the passenger-side door, and inserted my bag into a narrow space behind the passenger seat.

"We'll leave at eight," he informed me before rolling out the tarp on top of the shed from one end to the other, turning the space into a dark enclosure. "Why don't you come back inside the house with me," he suggested. "I just need a little time to tend to some final matters before we go."

I followed him inside, where he pointed out some take-out food he must have ordered from a nearby restaurant.

"I have California rolls and tempura here," he said. "I hope it suits you. I just didn't have time to inquire about your preference and took a chance."

"That's just what I would have ordered," I said.

He looked amused. "Let's go over the itinerary while munching our last meal, then!"

"Last meal? So be it." I sat down at the table across from him. "We'll first arrive at Baekdu Mountain in the year 2372 BC, right? Is that too far back? That's 4,392 years ago." I frowned, suddenly feeling concerned.

"Do you know," the professor said with a thin smile, "My machine has a max backward travel time of five thousand years. So we're well within the boundary."

I quietly blew out a sigh of relief. "And what is the speed of your machine?"

"It's adjustable, but the maximum speed is a month per minute, and we need the maximum for that far back," he declared, looking straight at me.

I fell silent, trying to calculate in my head what that meant for our journey.

"It will take us about thirty-seven days to get there," the professor offered, "including extra time for take-off and landing."

He had once mentioned that the travel time would be over a month, but I felt excitement anew at learning our journey's exact duration.

"Our body does not need nourishment during such speedy travel," he added. "Our metabolism halts and holds."

"You mean this last meal will take care of us till we land?"

"Exactly." He popped a California roll into his mouth.

The sunlight was fading when we finished our last supper.

Like I had, the professor turned off most of the electrical devices around his house and locked every door and window. At last, he rolled up the front door of the shed, pushed out Ray, and rolled the door back down behind the machine.

We climbed inside, and Ray slid away on the quiet street toward the oceanside not far from the professor's house. Luckily we encountered no one along the way. We rolled onto the wide beach, where still we saw no one around—and then, within seconds, we took off into the air.

Initially, Ray rattled a little; I braced myself until we had passed through all the layers of the atmosphere and reached a calm and motionless outer space. Now there was nothing, not even a swooshing sound around us, and my tensions eased. I left my fate in the hands of Professor McGordon and Ray.

There among the stars, the professor and I conversed at ease.

We found that we both had lived about a half century; we both were unattached then to anyone; and we both felt defiant toward a world full of silly conventions, stuffy pretensions, and foolish presumptions. These discoveries about one another made our journey considerably more comfortable. Relaxed inside our small craft, side by side, we headed forward—or rather backward—to the ancient world.

CHAPTER 4

We landed on a green patch near the bottom of Mount Baekdu, which soared into the sky above us, the highest mountain on the Northeast Asian continent. It was situated between the Korean peninsula on its east and the vast Manchuria plain to the west. The weather on the top was known to be treacherous, but at the foot of the mountain, the climate was distinctively pleasant in all seasons. *Baekdu* literally meant "a white head," and indeed the conical top of the mountain was all white; its ivory cap shone year-round and was visible from everywhere in the area. Baekdu Mountain was emblematic of the Korean spirit: haughty, aloof, ferocious, resilient, and at its foundation, pleasant.

The vegetation in the area was thick and abundant, and so were the species of animals. We saw it all as we landed.

I double-checked the gauge on the dashboard before I dismounted Ray: it said October 1, 2372 BC, as planned, the perfect timing for me.

The weather was at its best, sunny and crisp. The fresh air embraced us with its soft moistness and the strong fragrance of pine needles as we stepped out of Ray. I was ardently looking forward to stretching my legs.

As soon as my feet touched the ground, however, I collapsed without the slightest resistance. My legs felt separate from my body, as though they were not under my command. At that moment, they were simply two sticks dangling from my torso.

Much surprised and more embarrassed, I glanced at Professor McGordon. He had slumped to the ground in the same manner as I had, seeming to have no control over his body from the waist down either. We exchanged chuckles. All we could do for the moment was caress the ground with our palms and wait for our faculties to return to us.

The forest floor beneath us was covered with layers of freshly fallen leaves, under which lay damp peat moss patches. Grounded as I was, I looked up and around to see what came to my view.

The small green patch where we'd landed was a flat, rocky bed covered with velvety moss, and there were trees all around us, tall and majestic, silent yet powerful. They limited our views of the sky, and everything else around us was hidden by tree trunks, branches, and leaves.

"Do you know the names of these trees?" I spoke first.

"No, do you?" the professor asked.

"Some, yes, others no. Conifers, pines, firs, spruces, birches, and, ummm . . ." I chewed on my lower lip. "I wish I had researched the ancient trees in this region before I left."

"Are we on a botanical mission?" The professor gave me a wry look.

"I'm simply awed at what I'm seeing." As feeling returned to my legs, I lifted my bottom and stood up, wobbly at first, but firm soon afterward. The professor managed to rise at the same time.

We first searched for a place to call home for a while. We found a small, shallow cave with no other occupant in it and decided that would be good enough for our first days. It was rather a hollow recess, more a rock formation than a cave, but I liked that about it; a huge cave with a deep cavity would have made me nervous.

We gathered dry leaves and piled them inside our new home, then stacked the same atop our Ray, parked a few feet away. No one in this time would recognize what Ray was, of course—in fact, almost no one from our own time would, either—but we felt safer covering it entirely anyway.

"It's the day after tomorrow," I said as we took a moment of rest.

The professor raised an eyebrow. "What's the day after tomorrow?"

"The day when the sky opens and three thousand people descend from Heaven to build a nation—an ideal democratic nation—on Earth, the first of its kind in our history, the human history of the world."

At this remark of mine, his face showed nothing, and I was disappointed. How could anyone stay calm and cool at the prospect of witnessing such an event? Those three thousand people who would descend from the sky were the ones who would then build a great nation with a perfect government. Our history said so, and I had no reason to dispute it—and I had come a long way to witness it.

Professor McGordon remained silent for a notable duration.

"You're homesick, aren't you?" I asked him, sensing that there must be a deeper reason for his lack of reaction.

Still no response.

I needed to stay here for at least a year or two, long enough to see the mystic birth of Dan-Gun, the first king of our nation. If the professor was homesick on the first day of our mission, that did not bode well. But I understood, as I had experienced homesickness in America during my first years away from my homeland. That homesickness had eased as the years piled up, but it had never fully gone away; I had simply learned to live with it. "Aren't we all sojourners, Professor?" I tried again to engage and reassure him. "I adjusted myself to the American way of life, but not without pains and scars. In fact, I came to love my scars of homesickness."

He seemed incomprehensive of what I was mumbling.

I gave up. Perhaps he just needed time, alone and undisturbed.

At the close of the first day, we lay down on a makeshift mattress inside the cave, side by side. Whenever either of us squirmed in search of a comfortable position, it was counterproductive: any semblance of comfort immediately disappeared with the crunching of dry leaves around us.

After a few wriggles and twists, I felt the warmth of his hand on mine.

"Didn't I come a long way for you, Peonia?" he asked, his voice low. "When you first came to me, you gave the impression of a dainty, frail lady, yet you dared me to present to you my precious baby—Ray, the time machine!"

"I apologize," I said feebly, fatigue taking over my body and soul.

"No need for an apology. I soon learned that you're not an ordinary curiosity seeker. To my surprise, you quickly turned into a tough, determined, and resilient person. I've come to appreciate those qualities, and I had been waiting for a person like you to appear to test my machine. That's how I ended up here." He chuckled in the darkness. Without waiting for my reaction, he continued, "I am a scientist and engineer. I don't know much about history, the arts, literature, human psychology, or any of those non-science matters. You seem to be everything I am not, and I am drawn to that."

"We seem miles apart, but the distance between us is really as thin as a sheet of paper," I replied, thrilled but fighting fatigue. "We are the same, after all; what you are doing is what I am doing. We both pursue the truth of life, and we are both dedicated to this pursuit. We're one and the same."

"I don't exactly understand what you're saying." His voice faded into obvious exhaustion, too.

With no further talk, we both fell fast asleep, on top of dry leaves and under the single blanket we brought with us.

CHAPTER 5

The morning sun of October 2, 2372 BC, was bright, and sweet warmth softly wrapped around me as I got up. I brushed leaves off myself, stretched my limbs, and inhaled air thick with oxygen and pine scent. My surroundings were astounding, and I saw many things I'd missed the day before. I was again impressed by the magnificent trees. The scene's pervading serenity was often pleasantly disrupted by the flurry of movements of small animals through the tree trunks and branches.

"Are we at the point of the beginning of a civilization," I wondered aloud, "or perhaps at the end of a long-lost civilization from another era?"

The question of what to eat was soon taken care of, as Professor McGordon and I both easily located an abundance of fruits, berries, nuts, and edible mushrooms around us. After we gorged on the fresh delicacies, I explored the area until I finally found a spot from which we could witness the following day's big event: a small clearing free of trees and shrubs that would allow us to observe the sky with no obstacles in our way. .

When I returned to our temporary home, satisfied with what I had found, the professor was there, sitting on a rock the perfect size and shape of a stool, reading one of the periodicals he'd brought with him.

I grew overwhelmed with excitement about the coming event. *Would I really witness three thousand men trailing behind a young leader, pouring down from the open sky?*

Once again I briefly explained to the professor what he should expect to see the following day—the big day, for me—although I sensed his enthusiasm was not equal to mine. Then again, I had not seen him act thrilled about anything else; perhaps he just wasn't an expressive person. I gathered my courage and energy to effectively introduce our ancient world to him, our historical facts, along with the magical world of myth and legend.

I hoped that he would show some delight and elation at the end of my mini-lecture, but I only sensed his skepticism, which I did not appreciate.

Perhaps his mind is elsewhere, I told myself.

My excitement turned to anxiety. *Would all I hoped for really unfold before my eyes? Had I collected the right information in the last few years? What if none of what I had just described to the professor actually came to pass?* I was horrified by this last thought for a moment, but I soon recovered my conviction that I had the right information. My ancestors had been diligent in relaying and recording the facts of our history. All that was written in our history books was the fruit of the hard labor of conscientious scholars.

I looked up at the professor to see if he had come around and grown interested in what I was up to. I saw no sign that this was the case. I thought he must be savoring the success of Ray's performance. At the same time, he must be concerned about whether Ray would deliver our return trip as well.

I finally asked, "Have you ever wondered where you came from?"

"Hardly," he said with a smirk. "I know I came from my mom's tummy."

CHAPTER 6

I woke up to another gorgeous morning on October 3, 2372 BC; just as they had the previous day, red rays of sunlight glowed in the spaces between tree limbs.

The professor was already up and scrolling on his cell phone.

"Good morning, Peonia." His voice was cheerful, which was encouraging to me as I wiggled out of my piles of leaves.

"Good morning, Professor McGordon," I replied with the same cheerfulness.

"Oh, dear, call me Bill, please."

"Certainly, Bill," I said, pleased that we had reached a new level of familiarity. "By the way, are you getting anything on your phone?"

"In a very limited way," he said. "My cell phone does not seem to know I've brought it to a couple thousand BC."

"How about that!" I marveled. "I wish I had brought mine. I thought its functions would totally halt here. And how do you charge it?"

"It's solar-powered."

We laughed together. After a full rest, he seemed to be in as good a mood as I was.

I was well prepared to encounter this historic moment in person, and I could only hope that I had sufficiently prepared Bill, too.

At mid-morning, I led Bill to the spot I had scouted the previous day, where the view of the sky was unobstructed by trees.

Soon rumbling noises started rolling in from a faraway distance, approaching ever closer to where we stood; then thundering sounds boomed above our heads. The sky, thick with layers of dark clouds, came lower and lower, closer and closer to the ground over a place not far from where we were standing. I felt I could touch the cloud were I to simply stretch my arm up. But I kept all my body parts pulled in tight to myself, feeling that I should not interfere as I might provoke the anger of the mighty cloud.

Gusting winds swirled around us, tree branches

swayed, leaves on the ground furiously rolled back and forth, and the last ray from the sun slid into the scudding clouds, bringing near total darkness down around us. It was a dramatic and ominous scene—one befitting the great event I believed was about to unfold.

However, I was neither fearful nor frightened, as I had well anticipated this moment. I looked up at Bill and was happy to find him also calm, unintimidated by the sinister weather. After all, at our age, neither of us was new to surprises in life. Still, I reached out and grasped his hand, suddenly in need of some assurance of his protection. He gently squeezed my hand in return, signaling his understanding of my concerns.

I fixed my eyes on the sky. After half an hour, the clouds finally cracked in the middle. A small slit in the thicket of thunderheads gradually became wider and wider, its edges seeming to push each other farther apart. All noises and commotions subsided, and the sky was lit once again by faint rays.

I saw movements through the gap—and then, from the enlarged hole in the sky, a figure, an unrecognizable creature, emerged, soon followed by a myriad of look-alike figures, descending in single file.

Both Bill and I cocked our heads ninety degrees backward for a better view of the sky. The figures glided down toward us like giant birds, yet they were not birds. *The one in front must be the leader*, I thought, wrapped as it was in a loose-fitting white robe that flared and flapped around. At its heel, three unique and distinguished figures followed. I noticed that these three distinctive figures stayed close to the leader in the front at all times, and I assumed them to be the three ambassadors I had read of who received the royal seals of authority from Whan-Woong's father in Heaven, Whan-In.

By the time the gap in the sky began closing, I had lost count of how many figures had passed through it. After the last of the group emerged, the sun restored its position and the clouds moved upward, higher and higher. The sky was once again a clear and vast expanse, as though nothing had happened.

As the figures approached the ground, I recognized them as human beings, men and women. They lightly touched down with their two feet, their arms spread. All were wrapped in white robes, and all looked alert, yet benign and genteel. If the legend was true, there must be three thousand men and women here, led by the son of the King in Heaven.

It was easy to spot the leader, Whan-Woong, despite the size of the milling crowd. He had the look of a leader—dignified, noble, and confident—although he appeared to be only in his early twenties. I was hoping to also spot his father, the almighty King of Heaven, but did not find an elderly man with his stature. A little disappointed, I groaned.

"What are you saying?" Bill, still holding my hand, asked me.

"The old man, the King of Heaven, he did not come with these people," I said. "None of these men show the air of an old king. I had hoped to get a glimpse of him."

"Looks alone do not deify a man," Bill said mildly. "He may not appear any different from the rest of his men here."

"Perhaps true, but no one here looks old in the least." I sighed.

"I know looks are critical, but one can often be deceived by them," he said with a wink.

At his last remark, I shot him a big grin and got back to the business of enlightening him about my mission. My explanation had to be simple and quick, I knew, or his short patience on the subject would interrupt my grand plan to stay here with him for a while, a year or two. I cleared my throat and, while the thousands before us moved around, seemingly finding their proper place in the group, began my story.

"Whan-In, the father of Whan-Woong, governed the Kingdom in Heaven," I said. "He was a wise king, and his kingdom prospered. When his firstborn son came of age to take over his father's title and duty to rule the kingdom, Whan-In advised this son to rule the nation with utmost care and love for the people. The son assured his father he would do so and happily took over his father's realm."

Bill's forehead wrinkled with confusion. "Then, what's this all about, a bunch of people leaving their nation in Heaven?"

I was glad to hear him ask the question; it meant he was listening. "There was another son, a younger one, and—"

"Aha! You don't have to get into the details. Don't I know what it is all about now?"

I had not seen him so provoked before; I looked at him with great curiosity, waiting for him to explain himself.

"I apologize for overreacting," he said quickly. "I was in that situation. I was the younger one of two sons in my family."

I gave him a sympathetic look. "I'm sorry to hear that."

"What I'm saying is that sibling discord is everywhere after all," he said. "Please, go on with your story."

I continued from where I'd left off. "The father was deeply troubled. His true love was with his second son, Whan-Woong, who seemed better in many ways—more intelligent, more sensitive, even better looking. Yet Whan-Woong lived an aimless life, going off hunting day after day with no specific purpose. One day, as the father and Whan-Woong sat side by side, looking down on the Earth, it dawned on them simultaneously that Whan-Woong could have a nation of his own down there. What they saw was a boundless territory, uninhabited, thick with trees, plants, high mountain peaks, sparkling water flowing in gorges, and bright sunshine. At the very same time, they both stood up and chanted together, 'Yes, there will be another nation on Earth!'"

I took a pause to gauge Bill's interest in the story.

"It's getting interesting!" he muttered, clearly engaged.

"For three days and nights, father and son searched for the right spot to descend to. Finally, they found Mount Baekdu. On its east side were beautiful mountain ridges bordered with blue sea; to its west was the boundless terrain of Manchuria; to its north, a potential territory to explore for centuries to come; and to its south, golden plains perfect for agriculture. The spot had everything they wanted and needed." I flung my arms wide apart, emphasizing the vastness of the territory they discovered. "Upon learning of his father's plan to send his little brother to Earth, the first son was joyous at the chance to be rid of his sulking sibling. He had been troubled with his little brother around, sharing their father's attention and favor. He said to his father that Whan-Woong would do a great job on Earth and he would spare no less than three thousand elite men and women to accompany him there."

"How do you know all this?" Bill challenged me in the middle of my passionate lecture.

I smiled; this interrogation was a sign that he was getting serious about learning what I had wanted to convey to him all along.

"It's written in our official historical documents." Saying this, I searched my memory for the source. "Let me see—yes, it was in *The History of Three Kingdoms*, recorded by Ilyon, an official Chief Monk of the King's Court. I believe it was around the 13th century AD that Monk Ilyon recorded this part of our history. I also remember the same facts were found in a Chinese history book, *Jewang Woongi*, authored by Lee Seung-Hue."

"Good to know." Bill nodded brusquely. "Continue, please, I'm interested."

"By the way, don't get confused by the fact that there is also an epic called *Three Kingdoms*—a Chinese history—that is perhaps a lot better known than our *History of Three Kingdoms* . . . somewhat confusing, right?"

"Thoroughly."

"Anyway, Whan-Woong and his father personally screened three thousand men and women to emigrate to Earth. They confirmed the inclusion of three ambassadors—one for the Cloud, one for the Wind, and one for the Rain, the elements essential for successful agriculture. A ruler must feed his people, first of all." I stopped and studied Bill's face. "Are you sure you find this interesting? Should I go on?"

"Of course," he assured me, "I'm enjoying the story a great deal."

I was satisfied to see that his facial expression matched his words.

By the time I finished my lecture to Bill, every one of the three thousand troops on the ground had found their place in the crowd, and they were now lined up in formation. As I blew out a big sigh of relief at the fact that I had fulfilled my duty to inform my partner of the important facts, the group began to march downward from the mountainside, toward lower ground.

"Shall we join them?" I asked.

Bill nodded, and we positioned ourselves at the tail end of the procession and marched along with them. As I expected, no one seemed to notice our presence. I considered it a disciplined behavior on their part. The procession was methodical, precisely aligned laterally as well as linearly.

The objective, I assumed, was to locate a plateau with arable territory nearby where a town might be built. Indeed, I noticed the three ambassadors in front often halted the procession and looked into the distance in all directions, their hands cupped above their eyes. Fist-size jade seals hung from their necks, almighty symbols of authority. It was curious to me that their leader wasn't wearing any of those symbolic relics or ornaments.

I looked at the surrounding territory myself to see if I would select the same site they did. Instead, an awesome object came into my sight: a giant rock in the shape of an egg, standing alone beside of our path. It was twice my height and five times my width.

"Ah!" I let out a small squeal. It looked so much like a rock near my home five thousand years away, on top of the hiking course from San Rafael to Nicasio that it evoked a strong nostalgia in me. I immediately liked it and vowed to visit it again soon. I named it "The Big Rock," like the one above Lucas Valley.

"Are you saying something?" Bill asked, staring at me.

"Oh, yes. Do you see the rock over there?'

"Yes, I like it."

"We have the same taste. I like it too. It reminds me of that rock near San Rafael. In fact, it struck me hard, and I don't know why."

"It's your homesickness," he said wisely.

"Who do you think is the leader here?" I asked, changing the subject from the rock to Whan-Woong. It seemed almost impossible to miss, but I thought if anyone could, Bill might be the one, as he generally seemed uninterested in obvious phenomena around him.

"I'm not a good judge in reading one's status, but the guy in front seems to be the one," he said. "He looks quite different from the others and has maintained a position in the front this whole time."

"I agree," I said gleefully. "You are good. He is the one, Whan-Woong."

"Are you positive?" he asked.

"Yes," I said, beaming. "His face radiates nobility."

CHAPTER 7

Once we reached a flat area near the foot of Baekdu Mountain, Whan-Woong stopped the group's march. It was a fairly large, open space, full of rocky areas with grassy spots between them. Trees stood at a distance, holding their roots back from invading this area, as though they had waited for Whan-Woong to pick this very spot for a grand purpose. A roaring sound filled the air, sending us the message that clean water was available just a short distance away.

Whan-Woong had his men set up a table, which they carved out of the birch wood that was abundantly available. Another group of his men quickly carved bowls in various sizes out of the same birch. Some ran to the nearby river and filled the bowls with water. Other people busied themselves with clearing brambles and shaping the area into a suitable place to rest. I quickly realized that this was only a temporary resting spot, not the site where they would make their permanent settlement, as the rocky ground would serve neither their agricultural needs nor as a good foundation for the buildings they would need to construct.

Whan-Woong turned away from the table and bent down to wash his hands in a large bowl laid on the ground. I quietly crept forward to inspect the water in a smaller bowl on the table. The water was crystal clear, and through it I could see the fresh grain of the birch wood.

Mission accomplished, I quickly returned to my place next to Bill, at the back of the crowd.

Beaming at me, Bill whispered, "Must you inspect every detail?"

I nodded. "Why not!?"

A ceremony started. From where I was, I could not hear much of what Whan-Woong recited, but I recognized it as a ritual of some sort; he seemed to be sending thanks to the supreme being, perhaps his father or someone even mightier than his father in Heaven who was unknown to me. He then announced in a louder and slower voice that this new nation on Earth would be a nation for the people with equal rights, equal protection, and equal benefits for all.

Bill, who of course did not speak Korean, gave me a questioning look.

"Whan-Woong may be the first ruler in human history to invent and practice the principle of democracy of the people, by the people, and for the people," I explained. "He just proclaimed it."

"I'm sure if we looked hard enough, we could perhaps trace all the noble ideas and concepts of the democratic system as far back as the beginning of human history," Bill said.

"I agree."

Whan-Woong ended his speech with more ceremonial mumbles. He then lifted the small wooden bowl holding fresh water high over his head, paused a moment, lowered it to take a sip out of it, and then slowly returned the bowl to the table.

The sun was directly above us; I thought it must be noon. The ceremony finished, Whan-Woong led his people farther down through the foothills to lower ground, in search of flat terrain.

The sun was setting over the horizon of the Manchurian plain in the west when Whan-Woong's group finally found a suitable plateau with vigorous streams flowing nearby.

As the darkness of their first night on Earth fell, every one of the three thousand people gathered together, sitting on a grassy flat field with mighty Baekdu as their backdrop, encircling a bonfire that shot ferocious flames up into the sky. There was plenty of food to eat and fruit punch to drink.

When the meal ended, drums were pounded, bamboo pipes were blown, and the crowd started to swing their bodies to the tune.

Bill kept himself apart from the crowd, but I mixed with the people, eating and drinking and singing along, and no one asked me any questions. Eventually, I settled on a seat at the outermost layer of the circle and watched the merry crowd.

As the darkness of the night deepened, I spotted a set of sparkling eyes between the bushes and shrubs behind me. Looking around, I saw another set of eyes, and then another and another, behind us and around us in the thickets of bushes. They were the eyes of animals, I realized—not those of wild beasts with menacing ferocity but rather eyes full of curiosity about our mirth and merriment, eyes that revealed envy and a longing to join us. Obviously, these animals had not seen anything like this ever before.

As flames from the bonfire flared up high into the night sky, the sparkling eyes continued to stare at us. I felt eyes piercing my back, as though the animals were begging to talk to me. *Was it my imagination?*

I stood up from my seat and walked over to a bush, profoundly aware of the multiple sets of eyes following my movements. Still, I wasn't nervous; I sensed only intense interest, timidity, and even friendliness in their gazes. Somehow I was certain of my safety with these creatures.

"Would you just come out and join us?" I asked, beckoning them forward with my hand.

All the eyes retreated backward in a hurry to bushes deeper in the forest; none came forward.

"Well, I don't mean to frighten you!" I shouted after them. "Come back and enjoy our fellowship like you have been doing, please. I am your friend!"

The singing and dancing went on and on. Feeling very tired and failing to find Bill anywhere, I started hiking back up to our cave alone. It was an uphill walk, and it took a couple of hours.

"Bill! Bill, where are you?" I called out as I walked, but no response came.

I was concerned, but by the time I made it to our cave I was exhausted—too tired to continue the search for Bill.

I sprawled on my pile of leaves, pulled up our blanket, and fell fast asleep.

The next morning, the first thing I did was stretch my arm toward Bill. I felt nothing but a handful of dry leaves.

"Bill!" I called out. "Bill!"

There was not a stir in response, only dead silence in the air. I briskly got up and looked around, but I saw no trace of Bill anywhere. In fact, my memory was vague as to when and where I had last seen him.

Soon, an eerie feeling enveloped me, and it dawned on me that I should check on Ray.

I raced to the spot where we'd parked the machine.

"Ah! It's gone, and he's gone, too!" My heart beat fast, and my head spun—I felt like I was free-falling into an abyss, dark and damp. I collapsed on the ground.

A few seconds later, I recovered myself enough to look up at the sky, hoping to catch a glimpse of Ray.

Nothing was visible in the clear sky above.

I dragged myself back to the cave, feeling totally lost. I slowly gathered my belongings, as though I had a place to go. Then I discovered an unusual item where Bill used to sit in the morning, waiting for me to get up. It was a note, folded and weighed down by a small rock, partially covered with dried leaves.

My hands shook as I picked it up, but I managed to open it.

It's not without pain that I leave you like this. I saw that you would be fine, occupied with wonderful people and great events here. As for me, I realized I have a lot going on at the campus back at Stamperd; I can no longer be absent without risking irreparable damage to my job, career, future, and reputation. I left insufficient notice for a prolonged absence and must return to my office as soon as I can. You will find all my possessions at your disposition. I believe you'll use every one of them. Most importantly, I'm leaving my cell phone. It's a special one I made before our departure. Its use will be severely limited, but it may serve once or twice for you at a critical moment. I'll be back to get you sooner than you expect. Love, Bill

I sat immobilized for an hour. *Should I go on? Can I go on?*

I must have had the appearance of a ghost, all my blood drained by the shock I'd just received. Yet I mumbled to myself, "Look, he ended his note with the word 'love.'" It was the first time he had used that word with me, and seeing it there on the page, I came to believe he truly would return soon.

I did not want to see anyone, go anywhere, or do anything that day. In fact, I did not even want to eat. I just sat on the small rock where Bill used to sit, staring into space. I managed to look up frequently at the sky, and I watched the sun change its colors and position very slowly before finally setting on the horizon.

I felt pain all over my body, even after I told myself to let it go. "Let him go," I repeated to myself aloud. "Let Ray go, let your hope go, let it all go!"

"No!" a loud voice shouted back.

I looked around but saw no one. There was only me; it was my own voice speaking to me.

"Peonia," I said loudly, "hope and despair do not exist in isolation in life; hope is followed by despair and despair by hope."

The sun I had observed all day supported what I was saying: it was going down but would inevitably come back up tomorrow.

That first day without Bill, alone in the year 2372 BC, was the longest day of my life and the hardest one to endure, but it was also the day that brought my greatest awakening. I knew I must get my disorganized emotions under control.

I must go on.

CHAPTER 8

The routine of stretching my arm toward Bill upon waking in the morning stayed with me in the days following his departure. Every time, I touched nothing. It seemed he would appear from the bush at any moment, yet he did not. I got up and went to see Ray, although I had already checked the spot repeatedly and knew it was empty. Without fail, when I saw the hiding place vacant, I felt sharp pains all over my body. I stuck close to my cave for days.

A week later, two of Whan-Woong's people appeared at the entrance to my cave. They were very polite and invited me to their new town's center for that night's festival. They explained that the invitation was from Whan-Woong himself, and then they left.

I was somewhat surprised that Whan-Woong had noticed me or my absence at all, and even more surprised that he was inviting me to come back. *And how had they found me? Had they been watching me all along?*

I made my way to the town center before nightfall. Everyone was busy building dwellings and roads and working on other community needs, but they were nonetheless amazingly kind and polite to me; no one asked me any personal questions, and they all treated me as one of them, as though they had known me before, despite the obvious differences in my clothes and behavior.

I tried to return the courtesy by being cordial and friendly. I did not want to show my fear and sadness to anyone, so I pretended I was as happy and unbothered as everyone else. I wondered whether someone would approach me to explain why Whan-Woong had invited me there, but no one did.

As dusk settled in, everyone stopped working to set up tables in the plaza. They lit up the place with fires smaller than the one they'd built on the night of their arrival. I walked around to assist them with chores that were within my capacity, such as carrying around food trays and punch bowls. Soon, people began helping themselves to food and drinks, and I joined them without fuss.

As I was bringing my food tray and drink to a seat near the edge of the crowd, Whan-Woong appeared out of nowhere and walked toward me. "I'd like to talk to you," he said with a soft smile.

I had been expecting something like this to happen sooner or later, but I still experienced surprise now that it was actually occurring, and I suddenly felt apprehensive.

He guided me away from the crowd to a secluded area nearby. He took a seat on a raised rock, then gestured for me to sit on another stone near his.

The rays of the sun grew faint over the horizon, yet there was still enough light that I could see him clearly, up close for the first time. He was handsome, and an aura of nobility emanated from him.

"I am Whan-Woong, and you are . . ." His voice was soft, with dignity deeply embedded in it.

"Your Majesty, I am Peonia." I did not know if "Majesty" was the correct title, so I was relieved when he did not correct me.

"I know you are one of us, yet you are not one of us," he said, studying my face. "How did you come here?"

"I was just passing through this land when I saw you descend from Heaven. I decided to pause my journey for now," I said vaguely. "May I join you and your people?"

He did not seem to doubt my response, although I was certain that he had dozens of questions about me.

"Certainly, you may," he said kindly. "We welcome you to our community. I also saw that you have a companion, and he does not seem to be one of us. May I meet him?"

"In fact, he just left to return to his home."

"To his home?" He tilted his head. "Where is his home?"

"In a land far from here."

"Yet you decided to stay here."

"Yes, to be with you and your people."

"Well, then, I'd like to invite you to our council meeting. It will be our first one on Earth. Please come!"

"Your council meeting? Are you sure? I'm merely a trespasser." I was flustered, but I remembered my manners and added, "I would be honored."

"It will be in seven days, at about this time and in this same place."

He must have been reading my mind as much as I was trying to fathom his. He was neither hostile nor intimidating; on the contrary, he was warm and gentle, yet mysterious. He seemed physically younger than I had noticed in my first encounter with him a week earlier but more mature mentally than his looks would indicate. I was elated to be accepted by this community, and even more so to be invited to a leaders' meeting. The pain Bill had caused was somewhat mitigated by this turn of events, and I knew I would be fine here for a while.

Whan-Woong disappeared before I managed to fully express my gratitude for his invitation.

I gradually mixed with the people and did my share of community work, volunteering for small jobs. Spending time together all day every day, I became better acquainted with many in the group. I could tell they liked me, and I liked them too.

A week passed this way, and then it was time for the council meeting.

Only a small group attended: Whan-Woong, the three ambassadors with jade pendants dangling from their necks, and a few others apparently handpicked to be there by Whan-Woong. The agenda was well prepared, as I expected it would be, and focused on building their future in this area on Earth and establishing the community rules and order.

Toward the end of the meeting, Whan-Woong introduced me as a special guest and asked everyone to extend a warm welcome. All of them rose from their seats and clapped, and I knew that was a unanimous sign of their formal acceptance of me.

"The name of our guest of honor is Peonia," Whan-Woong announced. "And we shall call our town Asadal, the City of Morning Glow."

"Asadal, the City of Morning Glow." I repeated the name to myself, and it glowed in my mind.

As the meeting was about to adjourn, a rumbling noise arose. Moments later, a group of visitors marched in, most of them on four legs. Among them were tigers, bears, deer, rabbits, horses, boars, even crows, and many others—all the creatures whose eyes I had seen on the first night at the bonfire festival.

They all crouched, splayed their legs out, and touched the ground with their bellies, assuming a humble position before the Supreme Being they clearly perceived Whan-Woong to be.

"Your Majesty, we respectfully welcome you and your people to our land," a tiger said with a low growl, slowly raising his belly from the ground.

"That is nice of you, Mr. Tiger." Whan-Woong spread his arms wide. "I hope we get along well for years to come."

"We do as well, but we have one request to make on behalf of all of us here—a sincere wish," squeaked a rabbit, after hopping a step forward.

"What is that wish?" Whan-Woong asked.

"We, we, we . . ." stuttered a deer.

A fox made a wide circle in the air with his tail. "We want to be human beings," it said. "Will you please turn us into human beings like you all here?"

A wild horse trotted forward. "Show us the way to become like you," it said in a raspy voice, "so we can be merry, drinking, dancing, and singing around a fire pit."

Whan-Woong stood up and lifted his right arm high. "I see why you have gathered here. I highly commend you for bringing your wish to me. But let me tell you, being a human isn't always drinking, dancing, singing, and being merry around a fire pit. More often, we toil from sunup to sundown. More often, we have misery, pains, sorrows, and despair."

The animals shouted in chorus, "We know it all. We still want to be human beings—please, please!"

"Fine, I will consider it!" Whan-Woong said. "Come back on the seventh sundown from today and I will give you my answer." With that, he turned and walked away from the crowd into the night's darkness.

I believed Whan-Woong had a superpower effective over numerous matters, but I doubted that even he could turn animals into human beings. Yet he had responded by telling them to reappear before him in a week; what would he say then? I felt tense at the prospect of what might happen.

The animals, however, seemed thrilled by the response they had been given. They danced their way back into the woods, humming various tunes.

CHAPTER 9

Whan-Woong's people showed astounding talents in many aspects of life, including building quality dwellings at a rapid pace. They already had one ready for me to move into. I imagined Whan-Woong must have ordered them to prepare my dwelling ahead of the others.

I was glad to move out of that crude cave, with its dirt floor and dry leaves. Without Bill, it had become grueling to stay there, physically and emotionally. The day I was notified that my new home was ready, I retrieved my and Bill's possessions. Every single item had become more precious with the passage of time. I wished that I had brought a lot more—more of everything and anything.

Back down in the flatlands, I walked around the structure built for me, my new home. I was quite satisfied with the construction and a bit awed at having a place I could call my home in this faraway land.

Soon an idea for fun struck me. I decided to paint my new space in bright colors by smearing ripe berries over the birch wood panels. I gathered various berries in a container, smashed them, and set to work. The result was a simple form of beauty befitting the taste of that era. Everyone loved it, and many went hunting berries of bright colors in the middle of their working hours to replicate my efforts. Soon, the whole town came alive with bright colors.

Whan-Woong floated among us, exchanging nods and bows with everyone. Then he approached me. "I'd like to have your color work on my dwelling," he said. Before I could respond, he walked away. It did not sound like an order or a command, however; with his benign smile, it felt more like he was asking for a favor.

Of course I would not refuse him; it was an honor to be commissioned to the task.

I found his home on the edge of the encampment, larger than the rest. I started with his front door: the outer line of the frame with squeezed blackberries and the inner line with blueberries. I ran raspberries beneath the eaves, then pasted beeswax on top of the colors, exerting my by now well-honed skills. I was pleased with what I had done; it did not appear garish but simple and fresh, perhaps the best artwork yet produced in the community of Asadal.

Not long after I finished, Whan-Woong came by and inspected my work. He showed a broad smile of satisfaction and thanked me.

A few days later, a messenger approached me and reminded me that I was to be present at the council meeting that night, at the same time and place as the previous one. On this night, Whan-Woong would address the animals' wish to be transformed into human beings.

As dusk set in, I strolled over to the meeting place. That night's agenda was widely known among the townspeople, and many of them showed up. Numerous species of animals were also in attendance.

I made my way toward the front, where the three ambassadors and council members were perched on elevated rocks. Whan-Woong walked toward the round rock that stood higher than the others. All rose without being told to do so. Whan-Woong motioned to the crowd to sit down, so the people and animals settled themselves again on the grass.

With no introductory words, Whan-Woong launched directly into the issue of the night.

"I would like to see our people rule this region," he said. "The territory is boundless, so we need as many people as we can find. Now the animals desire to transform themselves into human beings. I have the power to grant this wish, and I welcome you all to join us. But you, my animal friends, must show the disposition and character expected of human beings if I am to grant you this transformation. You must earn this gift."

The animals and people alike extended attentive ears to hear what was to follow. Then the standing torchlights fluttered as a breeze passed by, making them, too, seem eager to listen to what Whan-Woong would say to the animals.

"I will give each volunteer a bundle of garlic bulbs and a pack of mugwort greens. You will take them with you into a deep cave where you cannot see the light. Live in those conditions for one hundred days. On the hundredth day, you will turn into human beings."

Without taking any questions from the audience, Whan-Woong turned and walked away, disappearing into the darkness. His aides stepped forward, ready to hand out garlic and mugwort bundles.

Some of the animals let out deep sighs, and their disappointment filled the air.

"Did he say that we have to live off garlic and mugwort for one hundred days in a dark cave?"

"Yes, that's what he said!"

"That pungent garlic? I can't stand its odor even for a moment!"

"And the nauseating mugwort!"

"Oh, what a cruel idea!"

"I give up—I can't do it."

"This isn't for me."

The air grew heavy and gloomy with profound despair. Even the people were disappointed, as they had wanted to see an increase in the population; everyone had been excited for the transformation to occur.

The torchlights were blown out by the breeze, one after another. No one bothered to rekindle them.

In the growing darkness, the majority of those present, people and animals alike, turned around and walked out, one after another. But some animals hesitantly stayed, and still others, firmly committed to their plan, stood straight and resolute.

The committed ones—a rabbit, a fox, a tiger, and a bear—walked toward the council members to receive their bundles of garlic and mugwort leaves. The four marched out with their staples in their arms, looking proud of their decision and determined to follow the rules Whan-Woong had set forth.

The four garnered intense attention from the onlookers. "One hundred days! Good luck!" cheered the crowd. "We will wait for you to come out as human beings!"

I had owned pets, and I knew of their desires to be human beings. My daughter's poodle, Tag, had wanted to eat what we ate, sleep where we slept, sit where we sat, walk where we walked, and ride in our car wherever we drove. I had always found his desire to do whatever we human beings did, a desire that I saw clearly in his pleading eyes, to be heartrending. I knew he'd desperately wanted to be one of us—a human being, nothing less.

I felt grateful to Whan-Woong for providing these animals a path to that goal, hard as the road there might be.

CHAPTER 10

At fifty, I was the oldest person in Asadal, and the people of the community treated me with great respect. They seemed to consider me an old, wise, and harmless stranger from a faraway land, and many expressed their desire for me to stay with them and not to disappear like my companion, Bill, had done.

For my part, I noticed not a shred of wickedness or treachery in any of them; they appeared pure at heart, obedient to their leader, and hardworking. To them, I offered listening ears, and I restrained myself from uninvited talking and readily extended a helping hand whenever possible. In return, they essentially gave me carte blanche to do whatever I wanted to do and be wherever I liked to be. I appreciated their love and trust in me. They apparently realized that where I had come from was beyond their comprehension, so they did not even bother to try to understand it. Whan-Woong was the only one, I perceived, who suspected I was from not just a faraway land but also perhaps from a faraway era or even another planet.

The day after the four animals marched into the cave they selected—one large enough to contain the four and not too far from the town—Whan-Woong appeared before me. "No one is to wander around the cave, and no one is to disturb them, such is my order here," he said. "But I'll give you the privilege of being near the cave. Keep an appropriate distance and do not interfere with their endeavors, but do please report to me any happenings you observe." As usual, he disappeared before I could respond.

"Gladly, Your Majesty," I said anyway, in the direction of his evaporation.

Everyone in town obeyed Whan-Woong's order and stayed away from the cave. Feeling privileged to be the one person allowed near it, I made it part of my routine to stake out the entrance for a few minutes each day from a vantage point a few yards away, behind a bush thick enough to conceal my presence. I made a point of not allowing myself to be seen by anyone.

During my first visit to the cave, I could not see or hear any of the animals, and I did not dare to enter to try to catch sight of them inside.

On the second day, the rabbit emerged from the cave, rubbing his eyes. Looking distressed and disoriented, he muttered, "It was terrible, terrible!"

I rose slowly from behind the bush and approached him to offer my sympathy. "I'm sorry," I said. "But it's been only a day, and you—"

"The pungent odor of the garlic and the nauseating stench of the mugwort are unbearable!" he screamed, cutting me off. "I have had enough of them. I'm done with it. I want fresh air and my sweet green grass."

With that, the rabbit hopped past me and away into the woods.

I reported the incident to Whan-Woong later that day. He listened with no expression.

On the third day, the fox crawled out of the cave, he, too, rubbing his eyes with a front paw.

"It was horrible, horrible!" he cried.

Spotting me arising from my crouched position nearby, he ran into the woods, hurling his one last shout at me—"Horrible!"—before disappearing.

I did not get a chance to say a word to him. I relayed that incident, too, to Whan-Woong.

On the fourth day, the tiger slowly walked out of the cave. She saw me when I emerged from behind the bush. Unlike the other two animals, she seemed to recognize me as a sympathetic friend and approached me looking for comforting words.

"Tell me all about it," I said softly. "Was it so hard to stay through?"

Still rubbing her eyes, she lifted her right paw and rested it on my shoulder. "You know we tigers are carnivorous; living only on garlic and mugwort greens will mean starving myself to death. Patience or discipline has nothing to do with it."

"Oh . . . don't feel bad," I said quickly. "It's all meant to be . . ."

"I'd rather romp through the vast forests and high mountains and rule the world as I always have done," she said simply and then slowly retreated into the woods.

I conveyed this incident to Whan-Woong. As he had with the previous reports, he listened intently but made no comments.

The bear was the only remaining creature in the cave. I continued visiting the spot and perched for a few minutes around the cave entrance each day, once in the morning and again in the evening. I could see nothing, hear nothing, and feel nothing from where I squatted.

Over time, my visiting moments grew shorter; after all, one hundred days was a long time. I hoped the bear would make it through the ordeal; I was anxious to see at least one of the animals succeed. I even harbored a faint hope that Whan-Woong might reduce the one hundred days to a shorter period.

CHAPTER 11

The cave where the bear was sheltering stood near The Big Rock—the one I had spotted on that first march down the mountain. To me this felt like my territory, my comfort zone. Every day, I scratched a stick against the rock to mark one more day of my watch over the cave. I then brushed my fingers on the rock's surface, feeling the rough sensations, which assured me of my ability to endure the crude life there. My daily duty of crouching behind a thick bush had become my moment of relaxation. There I could indulge in lots of happy imaginings of a life back at home in California—a life near and around Bill.

On the morning of the twenty-first day, I finally heard a sound from inside the cave. It was a sound I had never heard before, and I wasn't sure what to do.

"What was that?" I asked myself aloud. "Did I hear something?" I waited, and for the next few moments, I heard nothing. "No," I said, shaking my head. "I must have imagined it."

I was about to turn around and walk away toward the town center when I heard the noise for the second time—a voice saying something indistinguishable.

Suddenly tense, I stopped walking midstride and waited to hear something more.

Nothing further happened for the following few minutes. I resumed my walk toward town again—after all, the one hundredth day was still far away—but just as I did, the sounds of a commotion came from within the cave.

I spun myself around and exclaimed, "What was that?"

Listening closely, I began to recognize the noises as whimpers and light footsteps.

Is the bear walking around close to the mouth of the cave, or is it giving up, too, and preparing to leave? I wondered. I stood motionless and waited for the next development. I then heard a voice—unrecognizable, but certainly not the bear's low-pitched growl.

My heart pounded in my chest.

It took me a while to process what I saw next as a figure—an upright figure partially covered in clumps of dark brown hair moved toward the exit of the cave. Gradually I realized it was a human body, female, slender, and clear-skinned. Her gait produced a poetic cadence, floating across the surface of the ground with a fluid rhythm, one step after another. Clumps of brown hair fell from her body as she took each step toward the light.

As the woman emerged from the darkness of the cave, she stopped and shielded her eyes with her right hand, still partially hairy. She looked around, and spotting me, withdrew one step. Then she came forward again. I gazed at her with awe, and she looked at me, too. Our eyes met. I smiled and walked slowly toward her, my arms spread wide in a gesture of peace. She quickly withdrew again toward the darkness inside, leaving clumps of brown hair behind, but within a few seconds, she reemerged. Our eyes met again; again I smiled at her, and this time she did the same.

She was young—I guessed her age to be a year over or under twenty—her facial features were well proportioned, and her skin was pale, in contrast to the dark brown hair still falling off of her. It was a chilly late November morning; I realized she must be freezing cold, so I took off my jacket and threw it to her, and she deftly caught it. She seemed to know what to do with it, covering her naked body.

It had been only twenty-one days, far short of one hundred. "With only one animal left, has Whan-Woong changed his plan?" I whispered to myself. "He must have realized the necessity of changing the rule. He wanted to save one life, at least."

With a big smile, I took more steps toward her, slowly and cautiously. She seemed to perceive that I meant no threat to her. She smiled back at me and stood watching my approach. I kept my arms spread wide, palms facing up. When I was a foot away from her, she opened her arms, too. Warmth passed between us—and soon, we fell into each other's arms.

I found her body warm, her pulse beating strong, and her embrace secure. After a few moments, I released her. "Hi, I'm Peonia. Would you like to come with me to my home?"

"I thank you very much. I became what I wanted to be, but I am lost now as to what to do next," said the bear lady.

"I was determined to be like you humans in every way—the look, the way of speaking, and even the way of thinking. I plunged myself into studying your way of life from the first moment you all came down from the sky. I practiced what I saw and what I heard every day, including my days in this cave. Now I have achieved my dream of transformation, but I believe there is still much more to learn."

"Amazing—you deserve what you have earned," I said, looking at her in amazement and admiration.

We walked to my hut, and I let her settle on my cot. By that point, the workers had moved to an area far from my shelter, so we were not noticed by anyone. I handed her some garments and a blanket, and then I showed her my cupboard full of food. The honey, nuts, fruits, berries, and mushrooms inside were, I assumed, all her favorites, and I invited her to help herself. She just looked around in awe.

"I need to pay a quick visit to someone," I told her. "You stay here and rest until I get back."

After leaving the bear lady, I dashed to Whan-Woong's place to report to him all that happened that morning.

When I reached his hut, I requested a moment alone with him. His aides withdrew, and I stood before Whan-Woong.

"Your Majesty, I came here to report to you the bear's transformation in the cave this morning," I announced. "I counted it to be the twenty-first day. I happened to be near the cave at the right moment. I halted my walk upon hearing noises inside. A few minutes later, a beautiful young lady, still partially covered by patches of brownish hair, strolled out of the cave. I took her to my house, and she is resting there now. I am reporting the event to you as quickly as I could."

There was a moment of silence that seemed too long to bear.

"I knew you'd be the one to witness the bear's— rather, the lady's—exit," he finally said. "I'd like to call her 'Bear Lady' for now. You seem to be the most appropriate person to take care of her until I find a way to properly introduce her to our community. Will you please keep her at your place for a while?"

"I am happy to, Your Majesty." I began to slowly backstep out of his hut.

He raised a hand. "By the way," he called out, "make a daily report to me about her."

"Certainly." With this response, having reached the door, I bowed and exited the room.

Bear Lady seemed extremely happy to see me when I returned. I assured her that she would be safe and well taken care of at my place for a while, at least until she could be properly introduced to other people.

Once she had rested and eaten, regaining her strength, I guided her on a hike in the woods, thinking she must have missed being in the forest during her weeks in the cave. We managed to do this without attracting undue attention as we were careful to stay far away from the construction work taking place on the other side of the town.

Bear Lady indeed felt more at ease in the forest, and she romped around for a while, savoring her freedom in an open space; still, she said to me that she had no regrets regarding what she had done to herself.

We arrived at what was now known as Holy Hill, and she led me to the Holy Table where Whan-Woong had set up the first prayer ceremony on the day of his dive from Heaven. Bear Lady told me that she'd watched the ceremony and learned that one could wish for something at the Holy Table. When everyone left after that first ceremony, she'd dashed to the Holy Table and made her own wish to be a human being.

In the following days, I often found Bear Lady at the Holy Table, folding her hands together, still wishing for something.

"What is your next wish, then?" I asked gently one day.

She dropped her head, blushed, and stayed silent.

"It's fine for you to make more wishes, as we all do the same throughout our lives," I assured her. "You may get it, and if not, that's still fine, no harm will be done. I just thought that I could help you."

Still, she wouldn't say what she wished for, so on my next visit to Whan-Woong, I reported that Bear Lady was fine but seemed to have another wish and did not want to share it with me.

"Bring her here tomorrow, please," Whan-Woong said.

"Yes," I agreed, "I will."

CHAPTER 12

That early December morning in 2372 BC was crisp and chilly. I decided to dress Bear Lady in a better outfit; I wanted her to look as good as possible for her first audience with Whan-Woong. It was a challenge, as I had a meager inventory. I often wished that I had brought more of everything from home.

Given how few clothes I had, it didn't take much time to pick out a tan jacket, a white shirt with a collar, and a pair of black pants. After the final touch-ups to her appearance, I looked her over and smiled; she looked beautiful. I was proud to have her under my care.

We happily marched together to Whan-Woong's hut.

I was led in before him, with Bear Lady on my heels. I had schooled her in how to behave properly before an authority figure, so she stood straight, with her head slightly bowed, eyes downcast, and hands clasped together in front.

Whan-Woong observed her intently, his face impassive. He was the very picture of a supreme being.

"This is the bear lady from the cave, Your Majesty," I said, breaking the awkward silence.

With dignity, Whan-Woong said, "Bear Lady, I commend you for the patience and perseverance you showed during your days in the cave. You are now one of us, a human being. Lady Peonia has taken good care of you for the past few days, but you must learn to live on your own and become a productive member of our community." His voice carried a grave authority tinged with a bit of sweet grace. "Do you have anything to say, or any questions for me?"

"I have a question, your Majesty."

My eyes widened with surprise; this was unexpected audacity.

"And that is?" Whan-Woong asked affably.

"How old am I?"

"I've given you a year for each day you spent in the cave," he responded without hesitation.

"That means you are twenty-one years old," I informed her gleefully.

"Anything else?" Whan-Woong seemed amused with the bear lady.

"Yes," she said. "What will my name be?"

"Any suggestions, Lady Peonia?"

He had now used that word—"Lady"—before my name twice. I was quite surprised at this new, complementary title. Had I been promoted? I wasn't about to dispute a decision like that.

"Yes," I said quickly. "She will not escape being called a bear lady, so we might as well give her that name."

"I agree." He turned to the girl. "Your name is

Bear Lady, and you are twenty-one years of age," he told her. "I have found a place in town for you to move into. Lady Peonia, you've done an excellent job, and I hereby release you from further responsibility for Bear Lady. You may be excused. You, Bear Lady, stay and follow my aide to your new home."

"Thank you, Your Majesty," I said, and then excused myself.

Upon reaching my hut, I was overwhelmed by an acute sensation of loneliness. I missed Bear Lady, and I missed Bill. At first, I did not focus on which loss had inflicted more pain.

Then I admitted to myself just how much I missed Bill. What was he doing now? If my count was correct, he would have landed at home about a month ago—or was it two? I wished he had given me a choice in whether to stay here or go home with him before he took off alone. I would have asked him to stay just a few more days, and then I would have gone with him.

I heard his voice in the air: "A few more days here? I will not!" I knew it was only my imagination, but I looked around anyway.

It was true; he would not have been willing to delay his departure even one more day.

Have I become so attached to him?

Yes, I had.

I saw no improvement in my mood in the following days. I remained somber and sorrowful. Released from caring for Bear Lady, I had no specific duty to attend to. Everyone else worked without pause on numerous projects, mostly building structures, both public and private, as the city of Asadal quickly took shape. Without an assignment, I was no longer motivated to get up and see anyone. I stayed in my cot, constantly rolling over and repositioning myself in a futile effort to find a comfortable position.

My thoughts about Bear Lady became obsessive. *Why the bear and not the tiger, the fox, or the rabbit?* The more I thought about it, the more convinced I grew that Whan-Woong had pre-selected the bear to turn into a human being. He had known that the rabbit was too fragile physically, thus unsuitable to survive in a human world. The fox was too clever for his own good and would not make a sincere human being. The tiger was too ferocious, aggressive, and impatient. Of the four of them, only the bear was physically strong, emotionally tenacious, and wise. Whan-Woong knew what he was doing.

My thoughts circled from Bill to Bear Lady and back to Bill, where they lingered. I realized how little I truly knew of him, and he of me, as he had asked me only a dozen questions about myself and my life. But what did it matter if he was one way or the other?

The thing I most wanted to know was whether he would come back to get me. I felt almost certain that he would—but then again, what, truly, was certain in life? My predictions in the past had in fact more often been more wrong than right.

I caressed the cell phone he left for my use and wondered how many days would pass before he used it to contact me from California. I should hear from him soon—shouldn't I?

I heard a knock on my door and opened it to find a messenger from Whan-Woong.

"Whan-Woong wishes for you to attend his court as soon as you are able," the messenger announced.

I inclined my head. "I will be there shortly."

Within the hour, I appeared before Whan-Woong, who was perched on a high, newly assembled chair befitting his position.

"Good morning, Your Majesty," I said.

"Good morning," he replied in a pleasant tone. "I have a big favor to ask of you."

"Anything," I said.

"Bear Lady and I will marry as soon as we can," he said. "I believe you can help us with this event. I would like for you to organize her wedding attire. I would also like to appoint you as her guardian, so you'll walk her to the wedding altar."

Shocked that I was invited to directly participate in this historical event, I remained speechless for a moment but then quickly composed myself. "Congratulations!" I said. "It will be my honor, and I'll do my best."

"Can you do it by the next full moon?"

I nodded humbly. "I can, Your Majesty."

Whan-Woong looked down at me, beaming. "The ceremony will not be elaborate. I want a simple and honest wedding. I have much else to do for my people, and I do not wish to waste resources on my personal event."

"It's not just your personal event, it's also a community event, a historical event," I corrected him gently, "but I'll keep your wish in mind—a wish for a beautiful wedding at a minimal fuss, Your Majesty. The next full moon is about thirty days away, is it not?"

He nodded. "Precisely. I hope I'm not imposing on you—in fact, I have great faith in you. Now, Bear Lady will accompany you to your hut so you can begin planning together."

His aide brought Bear Lady to my side. She looked at my eyes, and her face broke into a wide smile. She looked even more beautiful than before. Hand in hand, we departed together.

At my place, I served honey, nuts, and fruits to Bear Lady.

"So," I asked as she snacked, "how is it that you came to agree to marry Whan-Woong?"

Blushing, she looked down. "I really do not know."

"But something must have happened," I pressed. "Marriage is no small matter in anyone's life, and marriage to a son of the King in Heaven is a big thing indeed." I cocked my head and waited for her to reply. I knew that Whan-Woong could not marry just anyone, much less a subordinate.

Bear Lady blushed again and confessed, "I told him that I wanted to have a baby."

"Wow," I said. "Where did you get the idea of having a baby? Do you know what it takes to have a baby?"

"I've seen babies born here," she replied with no hesitation.

Indeed, two babies were born recently. Bear Lady must have been attentive to her surroundings to be aware of such events. When she lived with me, I had been hesitant to explain such complex facts of life to Bear Lady; but in the end, I did not have to, as she had educated herself by paying attention to everything happening around her.

"I asked the mother who was about to give birth if I could be present at the event," Bear Lady shared. "The mother-to-be raised her eyebrows at first but soon agreed when I explained that I want to be a complete human being. I was frightened at first while watching the birth, but it was incredible, and I don't want to miss out on such a glorious experience in life." She ducked her head. "The ladies told me that I have to marry a man to have a baby."

It was the longest speech Bear Lady had ever uttered. She blushed yet again after delivering her fervent words.

She had surprised me at every moment since the very beginning of her being. I began to believe that she had been a human being in her previous life, and then had been born a bear in this life for some reason. I fell into a pensive mood, determined to unearth what had caused her to be born a bear when she truly was a person—a beautiful woman, to be precise.

"Do you remember your life prior to your birth as a bear?" I asked her tentatively.

She gave me a perplexed gaze for a moment, trying to comprehend what I meant, then shook her head.

I felt silly and told myself that I would not bring up the subject with her again.

She resumed her story, recounting how she had run up to the Holy Hill where the Holy Table was still standing in the center of the plateau. After watching the rite on the first day of the heavenly people's arrival and understanding what the ritual meant, she told me, she had repeatedly visited the holy spot, where she watched and listened to the wishes of many visitors. One day, she brought a bowl full of clear water to the altar and made her own wish: to bear a child.

Now Whan-Woong had decided to grant that wish.

I retreated to my cot for the night, and she settled herself on her own, which I had arranged in anticipation of her occasional visits with me. She was quiet, and I assumed she fell asleep. I lay awake, however, thinking of her reincarnation cycle. I was convinced that she had been a human being in her previous life. I began to draw pictures of her pre-bear life in my mind. She was beautiful and unstained by any human vices; then, I imagined, she must have encountered a situation where she had to commit a dreadful deed, leading to the demotion at her rebirth.

What could she have done? I knew it could not have been a truly depraved or despicable act because if so, she would have been reborn into a life-form far lower than a bear, likely a crawling worm or an insect. Given her beauty, I suspected that she must have been involved in a crime of passion. So far away in time and place, I felt that I was seeing a sister of the marsh girl, Kya—lovely, naïve, pure, and yet ultimately capable of committing a treacherous crime. In that story from my modern world, Kya was exonerated and lived out her days with her true love until her natural death. In this time, Bear Lady paid her dues by enduring days in a cave with only garlic and mugwort stalks.

She had paid for whatever she had done—that was what mattered. I wished her all the happiness in the world.

CHAPTER 13

The more I looked at Bear Lady, the more beautiful I found her. I informed her that the wedding would be a huge event in her life and her marriage to Whan-Woong would be a monumental blessing. She intently listened to every word I said. I discovered her to be a fast learner who absorbed and quickly understood many aspects of human life. The more I observed her, the more intelligent I noticed her to be. She deserved to be the wife of Whan-Woong, our First Lady, our Eve.

A messenger arrived at my door a few days later. He informed me that Whan-Woong wanted to know whether I needed anything for the preparation of Bear Lady's wedding clothes and whether I was running into any difficulties. I told him that I had everything I needed. Obviously, many things were simply not available. I knew I must make do with whatever I could gather within a month.

Additionally, I was not a skilled seamstress, nor did I possess much talent in creating anything beautiful; the only thing I knew how to do was sew fallen buttons back in place. *What have I gotten myself into?* I wondered. My limited talent in creating the bridal outfit was further curtailed by the absence of materials—cloth, lace, and fancy buttons. In the absence of these items, I selected the best-looking dress I'd brought with me, which fortunately happened to be white, and converted it into a formal gown by extending its knee-length skirt down to the ankle using fabric from another skirt, then spruced up my functional sandals by cleaning and polishing them. I next searched for anything that could be used as jewelry and ornamental headgear. As I had nothing suitable in my possession, pieces of animal fur—gifts from others in the community—played a big role in decorating Bear Lady's gown and shoes. It was wintertime, and I missed the luscious summer flowers and fall branches of gold and red—not a trace was left of them. In their absence, I gathered evergreen twigs and winter berries to adorn Bear Lady's tiara, which I crafted from branches, and to create a bouquet. I also made many other decorations by cutting out pieces from Bill's unused clothes. As I worked away, I complemented myself on how clever I was to have selected a sewing kit, of all things, to bring with me. Few decisions I had made in the past equaled this one. I must be getting old and wise.

Bear Lady remained by my side, watching every bit of work I did on her gown. When I finished, she was as pleased as I was with her new outfit for the occasion. I felt relieved that the celebration's food and drink were not my area of concern.

The big day came: January 31, 2371 BC. Whan-Woong's father in Heaven must have been watching the event and sending his blessing. He cleared the sky of clouds, wind, and rain; in fact, there was not even a hint of cold that day. The weather was incredibly gorgeous, brightly sunny and warm, an unseasonable phenomenon only Whan-Woong's father could have created in the midst of the unfriendly January chill in the Baekdu Mountain region.

As the time for the ceremony approached, the Holy Hill came alive with townsfolk milling around, all wearing their best and cleanest outfits, their mouths stretched into ear-to-ear smiles.

The groom, draped in a snow-white gown with no ornamentation at all, stood on a pedestal in front of the crowd, next to the Holy Table. His dark, straight hair was pulled neatly backward, without the help of any greasy paste.

I was delighted to have been given the honor of walking the bride from the back of the crowd to the stage. Bear Lady was radiant in her ankle-length white gown with animal furs sewn onto the trim, holding a bouquet of evergreen fir branches studded with bright red berries in her hands, and, on her head, wearing the tiara I had made of the same materials. She looked so happy that she seemed to float. Was she dancing? Was she flying low over the ground? Somehow her naturally graceful gait was poetically elevated by her joy.

When we reached the Holy Table, Bear Lady joined her groom, and I quickly retreated into the crowd.

Standing next to Bear Lady, Whan-Woong self-officiated his wedding ceremony. He lifted the Holy Cup with holy water in it, high up toward the sky. He mumbled a few words, then lowered it to sip a drop of the water before handing it to Bear Lady, who also sipped out of the same cup. There was no embracing nor kissing; they kept a one-foot distance from each other throughout the ritual. The groom uttered more inaudible mumblings, —and then the ceremony was over.

It was time to celebrate.

Everyone hurried down the mountain to the town center, a flat, grassy plaza, in the middle of the town's buildings. Musicians began to beat drums, signaling the beginning of the party, and the people soon started to dance to the drummers' rhythms. Gradually, we also began partaking of the food displayed on several tables: deer flanks seared on wood, plenty of fruits and nuts, and fancy mushrooms, lightly touched by flame.

After eating to my heart's content, I settled at the outer ring of the crowd. I felt satisfied with what I had done in adorning the bride. Mission completed, I wanted to go home.

I looked around for a chance to break away from the festival unnoticed, but just then, Whan-Woong sent a messenger requesting my presence at the head table.

The messenger led me to a seat next to the bride. I wished I had slipped away before his order, as I wanted to be alone. But since I was there, I drank the cups of potent fruit wine shoved at me, one after another, until I became jolly, then silly, along with everyone else. For once, my perpetually moody feelings dissipated. I mumbled to myself, "Am I going to stay here forever? Yes! No! Yes! No!"

I sat there until the groom and bride retired and the crowd started leaving. Only when the sun was a mere inch above the horizon in the west did I finally retreat to my home.

Upon returning to my hut, bone weary, I threw myself on the cot and immediately fell asleep.

CHAPTER 14

I had seen and done so much, far more than I had anticipated at the beginning of my trip. The next thing I wanted to witness was the birth of a male heir to Whan-Woong and Bear Lady—but only if Bill did not show up before then. The birth of our first king would certainly happen in a year or so, and I would be just as excited about it as anyone there. But that year would last an eternity for me.

What if Bill came to get me just before the baby was to be born—what would I do then?

Would Bill ever come back to get me? I recalculated the timing every day, estimating how long he had been home. I understood that he had much to catch up on at work and at home, but how long must he stay before flying back to get me? Had some unexpected issue arisen?

Though I had more questions than answers, I still firmly believed that he would show up for me. The question was *when?*

I had a strange feeling that he would show up a few days before the birth of our first king and not want to hang around even a day longer. If that happened, I would be torn about whether to go with him or not. A worse scenario would play out if Whan-Woong pronounced a decree to hold me and Bill there, forbidding our departure.

My extraordinary experience had apparently sharpened my senses, to the point that I developed a supernatural ability to see my future. I saw more than once the image of Bill at my doorstep, so I held firm to my belief that this vision would come to pass, and I grew increasingly convinced that he would arrive on or around the day of the birth of our king.

I was eager to hear from him, even if only a word or two, on that rickety cell phone. Finally, a message did indeed come in. My phone beeped, and the screen flickered, displaying the words *A lot happening here . . .*

I stared at the fleeting message on the phone, only to face the black screen again. The words danced in and out of the screen so quickly that I wondered if I had imagined it. I tried to respond, but my efforts were in vain. The phone would not send a return message, no matter what I did.

As winter deepened, furry animal hides regularly appeared on my doorstep—generous gifts from my neighbors. By this point, I felt well-liked by every one of them, and I felt affection for them in return. After all, human beings were yet to be contaminated with evil, vice, corruption, or treachery, so I had no reason to dislike any of them.

I had also grown accustomed to the simple, primitive way of life in Asadal, and I never complained about anything.

When spring of the year 2371 BC arrived, the three ambassadors—one for Cloud, the second for Wind, and the last for Rain—got busy helping people sow seeds in the fields. That summer, the green fields promised bumper crops. The people were happy and contented, and they multiplied.

Harvest time came, and then one day, Bear Lady showed up on my doorstep.

I welcomed her in. She was all smiles, unable to hide her joy. I suspected that I knew what that was about, and I immediately looked at her belly.

Nothing showed at her early stage, but she soon confessed the signs of her pregnancy, and we shared a happy moment together.

Soon after this visit, Bear Lady began vomiting every day. Unable to hold down anything she ate, she lived in misery, although everyone around her was delighted. I assured her that her nausea would soon go away, that she must bear it for just a little longer.

Meanwhile, she visited my hut often, as I encouraged her to do. She had numerous questions about childbirth and child-rearing, and she expressed her contentment whenever her questions were quickly resolved by my lively responses.

One day, soon after she left my hut, I went up to The Big Rock. The enormous, seamless piece was awe-inspiring. It never failed to soothe my turbulent emotions. My love for it continued to grow, and I felt guilty about defacing it with stick marks representing my days there, so I made them very lightly to avoid inflicting deep scars. Indeed, I made them so lightly that the first markings were fading, brushed away by rain and wind. Even so, I could still make them out. They showed that I had been in that ancient place for a few days short of a year. According to my calculations, it was now late September, 2371 BC.

I patted the rock. "Stand tall," I said softly. "You are the keeper of my sanity."

Two more seasons came and went. In late spring of the following year, Bear Lady sent her helper to my place to ask me to visit her. I guessed that she could no longer make the trip herself.

I went to her house and saw that her belly was enormous although I counted the delivery date to be early May, still about a month and a half away. A midwife had been selected, and the town was ready to receive their future king.

I refrained from asking Whan-Woong a question that was on my mind: *if the child turned out to be a girl, how would he take it?* No one wanted to talk about such a situation, and I would not be the one to disturb their beautiful dream.

During all the days of Bear Lady's pregnancy, Whan-Woong had talked about the coming birth of his son, the future king, and nothing else. He once told me that the first king of this land should be one born here, not an immigrant like himself. That cleared up my question as to why he had not crowned himself the first king of the land.

CHAPTER 15

As I sat on a stool eating my dinner one evening, I heard a brief static signal from my cell phone. I grabbed the phone. Like before, the letters sputtered, then disappeared, but I caught the message in brief appearances on the screen: *Leaving . . .*

That was the only clear word I made out before the message faded away.

It was around mid-March, 2370 BC, according to my calculations, and if he was leaving now, Bill would arrive in Asadal in early May, around the time of our baby king's expected birth, just as I had anticipated.

Of course he had to complicate things by coming during such a crucial moment.

Is he really coming to get me? Am I really going home? Despite the timing not being ideal, the message was the sweetest, most potent bomb ever dropped on me. Although not yet fully convinced, I felt buoyant, excited.

Then I questioned myself: *did I really want to leave this place? The happy people, the peaceful town, inspiring Whan-Woong, sweet Bear Lady who so loved me, and the soon-to-be-born king of our nation?*

These dueling wishes of mine became my psychological toy to play with whenever I was alone. *This or that? Would I send Bill back home alone, or would I jump onto Ray without so much as a courtesy goodbye to the people here?*

I went to visit Bear Lady the next day. My steps toward her abode were light and fast at one moment, heavy and solemn the next. I wanted to be with her as much as I could before my departure. Luckily, Whan-Woong had given me permission to visit her freely, and Bear Lady herself expressed her joy to see me every time I came, so it became my daily mission to visit her.

Finally, the day came. After spending so much time worrying that Bill's arrival would prevent me from attending the birth, I was relieved to not have to make a choice between witnessing this incredible event and going home.

When I arrived, a midwife was already attending Bear Lady, who was lying on a mattress on the floor.

Bear Lady was having pains at regular intervals. She looked up and gestured for me to come closer. When I complied with her wish, she grabbed my hand. Every ten minutes, she squeezed it harder, groaning each time. It was just the three of us in the room: Bear Lady, the midwife, and me.

Bear Lady's grip on my hand became tighter as the minutes passed, and so I went through my own share of pains. Her pains became mine—ours.

At the peak of the mother's painful screams, a second high-pitched cry filled the room as a new life came into the world. On May 2, 2370 BC, a boy was born. I later verified the date when I stopped by The Big Rock to read my own stick marks.

The midwife completed the initial wiping of the newborn and handed him to me as his mother passed out. He was a beautiful baby boy. Staring at him, I saw a halo appear around his head—it was not my imagination; it was real, and it lasted for about ten seconds. I immediately decided that I would keep this phenomenon to myself, however, as I did not wish to be identified as a spiritual being or a psychic, which I was not.

When his mother came back to herself, I carefully placed the newborn upon her bosom. Bear Lady dropped pearl-like tears, yet her mouth stretched into an enormous smile. I lightly kissed her forehead and left the two to adore each other. From now on, I knew, instincts would guide both mother and baby.

After leaving Bear Lady, I rushed to Whan-Woong, who sat straight on his high chair, pretending to be undisturbed, even unaffected. I reported the birth of his son, the future king of our nation, and deftly inserted descriptions of how healthy and beautiful the baby was. He thanked me three times in succession, which was certainly unusual for his personality, after which I, exhausted, left him alone.

I trudged back to my hut, filled with a sense that I had accomplished a huge mission. Moreover, after all this time spent with intelligent Bear Lady and noble Whan-Woong, I also felt sure that I was a descendant of the impressive pair.

Their baby, Dan-Gun, would grow up to rule an extensive territory, including the Korean Peninsula, Manchuria, and the Shandong Peninsula, for over one thousand years. He would then retire into the forest near the Holy City to live out his natural life. Historians would record his final years as a god or a god-like figure in the Holy City.

Dan-Gun's descendants would then rule the vast territories in Northeast Asia for centuries to come. There would be one great nation after another, one great king after another—all descendants of a son of the King in Heaven, Whan-Woong, and his wife, Bear Lady.

CHAPTER 16

The following day, a crowd gathered to celebrate the birth of their future king. They were in a festive mood, greeting each other with big smiles. Whan-Woong appeared before them and announced in a formal tone, "We have a healthy son, born to us yesterday, in our land, and I declare him to be the First King of our First Nation on Earth. His name is Dan-Gun, and our new nation shall be called Josun. Dan-Gun will rule us well, bestowing broad benefits to all."

As he paused for a second, loud cheers arose: "Long live Dan-Gun! Long live Josun!"

Moved by the spontaneous outburst, I joined in, "Long live Dan-Gun! Long live Josun!"

Whan-Woong raised his right hand high in the air and waved it in response to his people's roars, a big grin on his normally placid face.

Whan-Woong called me in to see him later that day. I was the only one before him in his room. This time, I had more questions for him, contrary to my usual passive manners before him. I hoped not to upset or embarrass him, but presented with this opportunity, I could not contain the series of questions that burst out of me: "What is the meaning of Dan-Gun? What is the meaning of Josun? When will our new nation start? When will our new king begin to reign on his own? Are you sure you should not make yourself the first king of our land?"

His beaming face remained benign, ethereal, and enigmatic, as usual. "Peonia," he said, "you have the answers to all of those questions of yours."

"Do I? How that can be?"

"You are an intelligent person, and you always know it all."

I gave this some thought, and finally nodded. "I'll try to answer, then. First, you want to set a rule that our kings must be born in this land."

He inclined his head. "Yes, I don't want a wanderer, someone foreign to our ways, to ever rule our nation, our people."

"And you would want to declare a new nation when our baby king grows into maturity, right?"

"Yes. The king will grow up, and as soon as he is able, whenever that time may be, he will begin his reign.

The counsel and I hope to be here, guiding him, until that time. Or even beyond that time, if necessary."

"Well understood, your majesty," I said. "I am particularly glad that you will be here until he takes over the rule of your people. You and your council will be valuable advisors. I also hope you and Bear Lady have a spare or two."

"We will work on the 'spares,'" Whan-Woong said with a smile, clearly amused, "but I hope you, too, will be near our baby king for a long while."

"I'm honored, but . . ." I looked away.

"But what?"

"I am homesick," I admitted. "I may return to my homeland."

This revelation was met with stunned silence. I sensed that I had chosen the wrong moment to reveal my plan.

Whan-Woong's body stiffened, and he stared at me. He showed disbelief at first, then surprise, shock, disappointment, and even a tinge of anger in rapid succession. "Must you?" he finally asked in a soft voice, perhaps in resignation.

My heart ached, but I did not want to deceive him. Again I said, "I am homesick."

Looking out through the window—an open, palm-size hole in the wall—Whan-Woong fell into a deep reverie, a long one. He seemed to have drifted into another world. Perhaps he was speculating about what my homeland might look like and how I would travel there.

Short of words to mitigate the awkwardness in the air between him and myself, I felt it best to retire quietly from the room.

As I retreated, I worried again that I had picked the wrong moment to tell him of my homesickness—*but if not then, when would have been a better time?* Bill would be back shortly, and when he arrived, I would leave this place. I could not do so without offering Whan-Woong some hint of my plans, not after all the favors he had given to me. Perhaps that moment would prove to have been my only chance to say a parting word.

I plodded back to my house feeling empty. Leaving these people would be more painful than I had expected.

But despite my mixed feelings, I still eagerly counted the days until Bill would arrive at my doorstep and I could go home.

I had not heard from Whan-Woong since our last meeting, which ended with his long, shocked silence. Had I enraged him?

I hope not! Nonetheless, I should pack my things, I thought to myself, *in preparation for my no-return departure.*

Then it dawned on me that packing would be quite simple, as I planned to take nothing home, nothing but Bill's cell phone. I intended to gift all my belongings to my friends in the community; every item, no matter how paltry and humble it might be in my own time, would be highly useful to many here. In fact, I wished I had more to leave behind.

I reminded myself not to overlook visiting Bear

Lady and the baby, despite Whan-Woong's possible anger. I worried that he would not want to see me near his beloved family—that he might even harm me in some subtle way if I came close—but I felt a strong obligation to let Bear Lady know my plans. She would handle it better than her husband, I thought.

Before my departure, I also wanted to find an answer to the meaning of the word "Dan" in the baby's name, Dan-Gun. I had already surmised what "Gun," pronounced as "Goon," meant: "king" or "the ruler." I also understood the meaning of the nation's name, Josun; it meant "morning calm."

I must get the meaning of "Dan" before I go, I told myself.

I walked directly to Bear Lady's place with no formalities, as none were imposed on my visits. By this point she was living in a new house built just for her and her son, a few yards away from Whan-Woong's hectic home, where people came and went throughout the day.

When I entered her front yard, I found Bear Lady baby-talking to her son in the garden. The early summer weather had invited everyone to spend time outdoors. I gladly joined her, sitting on a stool close to her.

She seemed happy to see me, as usual, and I wondered whether her husband had told her of my plan to leave soon. She did not seem to have any knowledge of it.

The baby waved his arms and legs vigorously in the balmy air. He looked healthy, and I felt good about that.

I had made up my mind to tell Bear Lady about my imminent departure—but seeing her broad smiles, I could not bring myself to do it. It seemed clear that Whan-Woong had not yet relayed the news to her, and I decided it would be better to wait a little longer to share it. I was certain that she would find it devasting; from the moment of her emergence from the mouth of the cave, she had shown consistent adoration of and trust in me. My no-return departure would be crushing to her. It was crushing to me, too.

I decided to put off telling her for as long as I could. After a brief visit, I took my leave and headed to The Big Rock.

My marks on the rock now showed one year, seven months, and three days. If Bill showed up here as scheduled, he would arrive in seven days. I vowed that if he failed to show up for any reason, I would remain standing here, next to this Big Rock, waiting for his arrival—or non-arrival.

I told myself that I would not mind lingering next to this magnificent piece of nature. This Big Rock reminded me of strength, dignity, and an eternity in solitude.

"Isn't that who I am, after all?" I asked myself.

But I hoped Bill would come.

CHAPTER 17

I taught Whan-Woong and his people Arabic numerals, which they hailed as a sacred code. Out of all the convenient devices available in the twenty-first century, I chose that particular concept to gift to them as thanks for all the wonderful things they had given me. I was certain that it was the right selection.

They put their new knowledge to immediate use by numbering the houses, starting with number one for Whan-Woong's and number two for Bear Lady's. They reserved the next eight numbers, then started at eleven for the three ambassadors, and again reserved the next seven numbers before numbering the rest of the houses. Mine was number twenty-one.

People were so enthusiastic about this numbering system that after they expressed the most obvious objects in numbers—like streets, distances, and the ages of people—they kept coming up with more and more things to be numbered. I grew a little nervous that perhaps I had revealed too much.

I could tell that Whan-Woong suspected that I knew a lot more, but I was careful not to spill any further information about twenty-first century civilization; such knowledge in that era would be at best futile, I thought, and at worst dangerous.

I wrote my house number on a scrap of paper and left it under a small stone in the spot where I expected that Bill and Ray would land, the same spot we'd landed on a year and a half earlier.

In the middle of a night within the range of my calculated dates, a knock came at my door.

I was wide awake, as I had been for the last few nights. I quickly opened the door—and there was Bill.

I grabbed him and jerked him inside quickly, not wanting to disturb any of my neighbors. His reappearance certainly would cause a stir—perhaps even inspire an intervention to stall or prevent my departure.

Overwhelmed with relief and excitement, I forgot how tardy his reappearance was. I forgot how much the passage of time had affected me. In fact, I forgot everything, including the words I had prepared to say to him.

Should I leave right now—quietly slip out of my house and be done with it? Or should I hide Bill for at least a day or two, and give myself time to say goodbye?

I did not want the town to know about Bill's return. I did not want to face the commotion, which could be a big one; I did not want to risk being held up from executing my long-awaited plan. But I decided I couldn't leave Bear Lady without saying goodbye. Besides, I quickly saw that Bill was in no shape to leave immediately; he was wobbly on his feet, and his eyes were barely open.

I decided to hide Bill for one day, enough time for him to restore his health for the return journey and for me to see Bear Lady once more and say a quiet farewell to her. To do so seemed my duty, and I had faith that she would not violate my confidence. I trusted that she would not block my secret plan to depart; if I asked her not to, she would not utter a word to her husband or anyone else. I was less confident about Whan-Woong's reaction, however, so I decided to avoid him.

"Just relax and catch up on some much-needed rest," I whispered to Bill as I tucked him into bed. "We can leave tomorrow night."

He nodded, his eyes already closed. In seconds, he was asleep.

As the morning sun appeared in the eastern sky, I strode to Bear Lady's house. I found her sitting inside, Dan-Gun asleep on her bosom.

I sat close to her but found myself unable to speak a word. She could tell that something serious was afoot, and just by looking at my face, without a single word passing between us, she appeared to sense what I was up to.

I wrapped both mother and baby firmly in my arms. Bear Lady stayed in my embrace without reacting at first; then she laid the baby down on a blanket and circled her arms around me. Teardrops rolled down her cheeks. I, too, shed tears. No words passed between us, but as sensitive as she was, no words were necessary. Her affection for me was obvious to me, as well.

We held each other for a few minutes longer. Finally, I loosened my grip on her, pecked her forehead with my teardrop-smeared lips, and stood up.

She broke into uncontrollable sobs.

"You knew I'd go back to my home someday," I said gently. "It is indeed far away, and the time has come. I do not wish anyone to know it, as we will all be sad, very sad. You know I love you very much; I also trust you. Please keep this to yourself until I'm gone."

Trying to hold back her tears, she nodded. What a noble face she showed as she assured me I could trust her.

I lightly touched the baby's forehead with my lips and left.

Bill was in a sound sleep when I returned to my hut; perhaps he had been the whole time I was gone. I told myself that we had better wait till nightfall before leaving.

That day was the longest of my entire life. We did not share a single word even after Bill finally woke up because the structures were not soundproof and I did not wish to take any risks.

Finally, a moonless night covered the world around us. We quietly walked up the hill to where he had parked Ray, my hope. We still did not say a word; we simply settled inside Ray and took off.

CHAPTER 18

During the first days on Ray, we spoke very little, as I spent most of my waking hours deep in thought about the land and people I had left behind. Bill let me be during those silent days as Bear Lady, Whan-Woong, the baby, and the rest of the people of Asadal danced around the inside of my head, my heart, and my body. All of them surrounded me in layers, leaving no room for anyone or anything else to enter my mind.

The whole town would discover my disappearance soon, if they hadn't already, and they might realize that it was irreversible. I hoped Whan-Woong would not feel betrayed and that Bear Lady did not blame herself. I also hoped that the townspeople would not point their fingers at her. I even hoped that no one in town had observed me entering or exiting her house on the day of my disappearance; hopefully they would not discover that Bear Lady had any knowledge of my departure before I left. She had obviously kept her promise; if she had not, Whan-Woong would likely have sent his men to detain me, or at least have demanded a last word with me.

Bill seemed to understand and accept that I was mourning the abrupt loss of my community. He remained silent throughout the long hours, for several days.

Finally, on the fourth day, I opened up. "Thank you for coming to get me out of . . . uh, out of the unreal world," I said. "There were times when I believed I would be stuck in that place forever. I saw myself standing on the hillside, waiting and waiting for you to show up, finally becoming a petrified rock there."

"I'm so sorry it took me so long to come back," he said. "There was a lot to catch up on in my office. After all, the first trip was almost a three-month-long absence with short notice and a poor explanation—enough to foment serious suspicion among my colleagues. I told them I had had COVID, but that excuse didn't stretch very far."

"I understand, and there's no need for an apology," I said. "You are here now. That's all I want and all I need."

"How about things there? All went well?"

"Yes. Things could not have gone better, and it was all thanks to you."

"We'll have more than enough time here in this cabin for you to tell me everything. Shall we start?"

I nodded. "It was all so unreal!"

I took a deep breath to prepare myself to tell the long, long story.

I started with the people's acceptance of me into their world through Whan-Woong's initiation. "That was the right beginning, and all that followed flowed naturally: my attendance at their council meetings, witnessing a bear transform into a woman, the wedding of the bear-woman to Whan-Woong, and the birth of our first king from their union."

Bill listened intently to all this. "Wonderful!" he marveled. "It sounds like I came back at the right time!"

"Indeed, you did." I couldn't agree more with that. I paused for a few minutes, feeling overwhelmed and enthralled again by the fact that he'd shown up.

He tilted his head and asked, "But didn't you want to see the little one grow up and become a king, the first one in your history, and rule the world as you've been claiming, Peonia?"

"Yes, I would have loved to see him grow and become a king, a wise one," I admitted. "But history says that he became a king at the age of thirty-seven. I would not have lived long enough to see it."

Bill showed surprise. "Why at the age of thirty-seven? That seems very late!"

I shrugged. "Perhaps Whan-Woong was being extra cautious, wanting to ensure that our first nation would be mistake-proof. Or perhaps Dan-Gun showed maturity late in his life."

"I think I understand the situation," Bill said. "My father took a long time to trust me to be a responsible man."

"You and Dan-Gun are lucky to have such attentive fathers," I said wistfully.

"Do you mean your father was otherwise?"

"My father didn't care one way or the other." My voice took on a bitter edge. "I was on my own."

Bill seemed bemused by my change of tone, which saddened me. I quickly switched our conversation back to the subject of the epoch I had just visited.

"Bear Lady's last teary face will not leave me; it's glued to my mind," I said. "I felt so bad leaving, as she was truly attached to me; she seemed genuinely disheartened to see me go."

"Don't you think we run into such a situation more than once in our life?" Bill stroked his chin thoughtfully. "Our lives are full of more sorrows of parting than joys of meeting, and more of the grievances of losing than the pleasures of gaining."

"Wow! What a powerful meditation on life!" I beamed at him. "It's nice to finally hear you talk philosophy. I knew all along that you weren't just a dry scientist; you are a great thinker on matters of life and death as well. Do tell me, please, what you've done since you ran away alone from Mount Baekdu."

"I did not run, I walked to Ray," he said wryly. "Anyway . . . I had a lot to explain to the school. I almost lost my job. My absence was long, and my explanation was short. The less I talked, the better, though, I figured. I properly secured a three-month leave of absence this time. I hope my return to work after we get back will not cause so much uproar among my colleagues."

"I wonder, what exactly did you say to them after the first trip, and what will you say this time?"

"I tried to avoid saying much at all, which made them suspicious. Some even suggested I eloped with a secret sweetheart, ha, ha . . ."

"That's a whole lot better than the truth!" I said, laughing.

"Peonia, you tell me, what would have been the magical words to get me out of trouble? I'd like to know because I'm sure I'm still not done explaining my last disappearance."

"I take my words back," I joked. "They guessed it right. Indeed, you ran away with a secret sweetheart. Isn't it true?"

We burst into laughter together, letting all our worries evaporate into the firmament.

CHAPTER 19

Bill must have engineered things so we would land at an early hour, in the dark, thereby avoiding unwanted attention. We landed deep in the woods on a mountainside near Silicon Valley, like we had at Baekdu Mountain. Bill was adamant about not being seen or heard, which I perfectly understood.

After carefully covering Ray with twigs and branches, we hiked down to a town, arriving at dawn. We were able to escape undue curiosity from early morning joggers as we were not dragging any suitcases behind us; between the two of us, we carried only a couple of thin credit cards, a few dollar bills stuffed into our trouser pockets, and the cell phones.

Bill called two Ubers for us, and both appeared within minutes. Without much fuss or any big parting gestures, we each headed in our own direction.

I entered my house after an absence of almost two full years, uncertain of what I would find. The furnishings remained intact but had collected generous piles of fine dust. The air felt different, and it smelled stuffy and musty.

I opened all the doors and windows, but then I felt I could not do anything else, much less clean. I did not have the energy. Instead, I threw myself onto the sofa in the living room, raising a mushroom cloud of dust, and stayed there unmoving for the whole first day, the silence my only companion.

Returning to myself in the current year seemed as difficult as adjusting to the lifestyle of five thousand years ago. I could not bring myself to do anything except lie on the couch day after day. I preferred to let myself be free from all of the obligations of modern life. Nothing mattered.

Finally, one thought motivated me. There was one thing I had to do: memorialize my experience, my priceless contact with that ancient time. No matter how enormous the task might prove to be, I knew I must do it.

I also realized that I needed to collect as many materials as possible about Dan-Gun's life.

In the course of my research, I learned that there were official records of King's Court documents of the Goryo Dynasty (918–1392 AD), better known as "Korea" today, still in existence. An official court monk named Ilyon had collected discarded historical documents and written a book called *The Overlooked Records of the Three Kingdoms*. Monk Ilyon was known to be a diligent and credible scholar in his time, and he had no motive to fabricate the story of "Bear Lady." Indeed, what Monk Ilyon had recorded, I had witnessed.

Should I have taken writing pads and pens with me to Asadal? I'd thought they would be more of a hindrance than a help. I had wanted my life there to be unhampered and uninterrupted by constant urges to jot things down. In addition, writing everything down would have put me at risk of being exposed and likely suspected of being a spy from an unknown place or a being with superhuman powers. Additionally, I hadn't wanted to deal with copious volumes of documents. I had concluded that it would be better to simply concentrate my attention on observing the first people's daily lives and to bring back just memories, nothing else.

I wanted to be a fiction writer, not a reporter; I wanted to create a painting of the world I had visited, not take a photo. I would paint a grand scene on a canvas, using my memories as my tools.

I felt a need to call Bill. He answered on the second ring.

"Well," he said, "you must have read my mind. I was about to call you, and you beat me by two seconds."

"Two seconds are a long time," I joked. "Anyway, here I am, just wanting to know how you're doing."

"I'm fine, and you?"

After that first call, Bill and I spent time together often, and those moments were happy ones for me. I was not at all scientific and he not at all artistic, but these opposing elements may have been the secret formula for the spark in our relationship. I talked about Mozart, Chopin, Van Gogh, and Cezanne; he shared with me his designs, models, constraints, projects, and tests. There were times when the clash of our conversation topics bothered us both a little, but we quickly grew to enjoy listening to one another talk about our divergent tastes, dispositions, inclinations, and habits. Above all, our journey to five thousand years ago was a unique and invisible force that bound us tightly together. We became inseparable.

Until the day Bill called me to say that he could no longer see me or contact me in any way going forward.

The call was short and terse, and Bill gave no reason for his decision; in tone and brevity, the communication resembled a lay-off notice to a factory worker. I was devastated. I was not, however, about to pursue explanations from him. I was determined to let it be, no matter how much it hurt. I knew all too well that life was full of bitter and sweet surprises. This was one of the bitterest.

I tried to reframe his rejection as a chance for me to dive into writing my memoir without delay or interruption. Such focus did mitigate my pain. I kept telling myself that I had a bigger mission—bigger than spending sweet moments with sweet Bill. Time helped me heal, and I seemed to have entered a new phase of my life, happily occupied with my project. Months passed without a word from Bill while I wrote and wrote, creating a record of my extraordinary involvement in the past.

I was deep in my writing when a buzz on my cell phone called my attention—strangely, that buzz out of all the other buzzes compelled me to look, and when I did, I saw that I had a text message from Bill.

I want to see you as soon as you are free.

I stared at it for a few seconds. All my pain over our abrupt breakup months earlier came alive, and I hesitated to respond. I had driven him out of my tender heart and planned to never see him again. Yet my resolve was weak.

When? I wrote back.

Now, he replied.

When we sat down across from each other at a round table in a coffee shop, we looked at each other slowly. His gentle, sweet smile immediately melted all the doubts and anger piled up in my heart.

He was the first one to speak: "How have you been?"

Only then did it dawn on me that Bill must have disconnected himself from me for a reason. I was eager to hear him explain. While I remained uncommitted to answering his question, he opened up.

"I'm sorry. I can't be with you for very long today, but I didn't think I could leave you in the dark any longer," he said in a low voice. "Paparazzi have been following me around. They smell a connection between my absences and my time machine."

"Wow!" My eyes widened. "I hope you're handling the situation well."

"It has not been easy." He sighed. "I had to try to explain my two long absences, and the whereabouts of my machine. They mentioned my 'funny-looking car,' and how it's missing from my shed—at least one of them must have snooped there during one of my travels back in time. Now, after finding me but not my machine, they are demanding explanations. I've said nothing about you, but I'm still afraid they may somehow connect your disappearance to the machine, too."

"Not possible!" I declared. "I'm far from being a celebrity worth tracking down." Scowling, I continued, "Snooping in your shed is clearly illegal, and they can't come forward with information they've illegally obtained." If they blabbered, they would be admitting to their criminal act.

"If they reach you somehow, you know what to say," he responded. "Please deny everything. I don't want any publicity yet. Not that I am guilty of anything, I just don't want to be hounded and forced to reveal my formula for our Ray."

He stood. "Wait till you hear from me. Be patient. Deny everything to all paparazzi if you're ever discovered, and leave no trace of our connection—no texting, no phone calls, no emails, please." With that, he hurried out to his car.

"Don't worry at all about me," I shouted at his

back—but in a voice barely louder than a whisper, lest anyone should notice.

I walked over to the counter and ordered another cappuccino with this question spinning in my mind: *What if someone does contact me and questions my long absence or my relationship with Bill?*

It all would be quite aggravating and annoying. I could say, "None of your business!" But that would trigger a sharp curiosity. I patted my own back for a least not having shared anything about my experiences with anyone yet. No one knew I had journeyed five thousand years into the past, nor did anyone know I had met a man recently. Long silences from me were not considered unusual by my friends and relatives, and now I was especially glad that was how I lived.

I stayed home the following week, avoiding social contact as much as I could. I had plenty of things to do at home in any case, in addition to my writing project. I paid keen attention to the current news, local and national, watching for stories about Bill or his machine. None surfaced, as far as I knew.

One day, I found a small surprise in my mailbox: a greeting card addressed to me. It had no return address, but I opened it anyway.

This may be the safest way to communicate with you. I am still hounded by reporters constantly. They keep asking questions about whether I've ever been on my time machine, whether I've traveled to the future or to the past. I am not ready to discuss any of that with anyone, now or ever. B.

I refrained from responding to him, trusting he would understand my choice to remain quiet. His wish to remain undisturbed was my wish too. I hid the greeting card from Bill—with the same extra effort I was making to keep my memoir away from any and all of my acquaintances. Certainly, with all that was happening, publication of my work would have to wait.

The next week, devoid of any communication between Bill and myself, seemed to last an eternity. Then I had an idea.

That afternoon, I dropped a holiday greeting card in the mail, adding no return address and saying nothing other than *Happy Holidays to you and Ray!* There was no holiday around that time, but it would serve my purpose.

Simply waiting for the passage of time seemed to be the only option for us. I had no doubt that Bill would take good care of himself, and I had no problem keeping myself occupied in the meantime; I was fully enmeshed in my own project. For now, I was content to lead a private life in seclusion.

CHAPTER 20

Several months passed without any noteworthy events taking place. I finally began to relax my vigilant ways, having concluded that all must be settled. Therefore, it came as a shock when I suddenly saw Bill's photograph in the local newspaper.

What's going on? I wondered, scanning the page.

Accompanying the photo was an article about Bill, written by a reputable reporter.

My peace shattered, my body shaking slightly, I managed to read it.

Professor Willard McGordon of Stamperd University created a working time machine, but he is no longer in possession of it. After determining that the machine would serve no good purpose for humanity as a whole,

the professor destroyed the machine. He has decided
that he would rather work on other projects. He is now
developing a spaceship to reach another planet, rather
than another epoch.

The reporter went on to say that he was convinced by Bill's explanation and looked forward to witnessing his next invention.

I chucked the paper on the floor and stared into the ceiling from the sofa. *Did Bill really believe the time machine served no useful purpose for human beings? Had he really destroyed Ray?*

I felt a powerful urge to see him, to talk to him, to understand his actions. But my fear of getting caught by the reporters, just when things were wrapping up tidily, was stronger.

I convinced myself to abandon my desire; it would be far too imprudent to see him so soon after this article was published.

Bill sent me another note, handwritten. He was obviously worried that writing anything on his computer, which was likely interconnected with other units in his school, would be too risky. The note said that he would like to see me at a certain time and place. Despite my earlier restraint, I was only too happy to comply and eagerly made my way to see him.

We met on the sidewalk in a neighborhood near my house, not far from some restaurants. While I was choked up, overcome with joy and relief, when I saw Bill, his face remained impassive, showing little sign of the pressure he had recently been under.

"Good to see you, you're looking good!" he greeted me cheerfully.

"You as well," I mumbled, overcome by the moment.

We started walking side by side, and he launched immediately into an explanation of what had happened since our last meeting. "My second absence really raised the reporters' suspicions," he told me. "Since my return, they have been hanging around my office on campus and around my house and neighborhood. Luckily, I had the machine stowed away deep in the mountainside, as you know."

I nodded. "What do they want to know?"

"They want to see my machine, to know if it's real—and if so, have I used it? Where did I go? What did I get from the trip?"

"And your responses were . . . ?"

"No, no, nowhere, nothing."

I winced. "And do you mean that?"

Bill took a deep breath and blew out a big sigh. "I don't want another trip."

"Are you saying that you regret the trip you took with me?"

"I'm saying that I do not want another trip."

His tone of voice told me not to further pursue the matter or else. I got the message but wondered how he had arrived at that conclusion when I thought things were going well for him and for me and for Ray. Not wanting to engage in a squabble, however, I shut up, and an awkward silence ensued.

"I have thought a lot about this over the last few months," Bill finally said.

"And?"

"I don't think my time machine will serve any good purpose for the majority of human beings. It served you alright, but I find it hard to believe that anyone else would greatly benefit from travel to the past."

"How so?"

"I don't want to deliver a slap to archeologists, excavators, historians, researchers, and other serious scholars who dig and dig into our past. If we can visit any time period we like, what use are their efforts? Let their noble jobs survive."

This left me speechless. Perhaps he knew what he was saying—perhaps he was even correct in thinking so. But I still could not make peace with his decision to put Ray out of commission.

"Let the past be the past," Bill said seriously.

While considering his words, I came up with my own: "Your machine lifted the fog on our history. Isn't that a worthy purpose?"

"As I said, my machine served you fine—but no more." He stole a sideways glance at me as we continued to walk beside each other. "Benefits in other instances would not necessarily be worth the trouble or the risk. And the beauty of research is peering through the fog into our past, precisely because we do not have a clear picture. The fog is what keeps scholars arguing. They love to argue."

I did not agree, and a dead silence fell between us.

"While scholars argue about the foggy pictures of our past, let's eat," I finally said. "I'm hungry."

This offer to enjoy a meal together changed both of our moods for the better; we seemed to have pulled ourselves back from the brink of disaster, from the prospect of endless arguing and being turned off by each other.

As we headed to a nearby restaurant, however, I found that I could not shake off what Bill had said about his time machine and our trip. At least for the time being, though, I wouldn't let myself protest his intention to destroy Ray.

We enjoyed our meal without uttering a single word on this forbidden subject.

CHAPTER 21

At home, I did my best not to think of Bill's words about Ray, but I couldn't help it. *Wouldn't it be splendid*, I thought, *if we could visit King Tut, Helen of Troy, King David, Cleopatra, King Arthur, and all those great historymakers in the remote past?*

On the other hand, perhaps he was right that what we knew would suffice. What happened in the past had happened. We have already gleaned vital lessons from all that we already know of the past. We should move on—I should.

A week later, Bill asked me to see him again. Of course, I agreed. We met in the same place as before.

"I'm free now, completely," he announced as we fell into step next to each other.

"What do you mean?" I asked.

"No one is interested in my machine," he said gleefully. "No one is after me now."

"Did anything in particular happen?"

"I told the most persistent paparazzo that I had destroyed my model and that no part of the machine exists anymore. He believed me, finally."

"What did you really do with Ray?"

"It's not there anymore," he said, waving a hand in the air. "It's not anywhere now."

I gave him a puzzled look. "How is that?"

"Over the last few months, every week I hiked to where I hid Ray and disassembled it piece by piece, each time stuffing the newly removed pieces into my backpack, bringing those down to my house, and dumping them in the garbage bin. It's all gone now. I'm free of it all."

I was speechless, my mouth agape and my eyes fiery. That precious machine was no more. "That was a miracle in human history, and you destroyed it," I sputtered. "I can't believe you did that!"

"I'm the one who created it," he said with a shrug.

"Of course," I said tersely, "but once such a rare commodity is born, it belongs to our society, like the telephone, train, automobile, computer, and all those other technologies that we all benefit from. You shouldn't have destroyed it." After a pause, I continued,

"If you don't like to travel to the past, you could travel to the future, right?"

"Yes," he said, "but wouldn't the world, then, become a dangerous place to live in?"

"How so? Wouldn't the world be a better place if we could anticipate disasters and do something to prevent them?"

"Intellectual predictions about our future will suffice," he said. "We should not go there and actually see our future ahead of time. Many learned people—wise men, religious leaders, even politicians—predict our future, but predictions are just predictions, not facts. Predictions are guessing, no matter how well calculated they are; they can never be equal to seeing something with your own eyes."

"That's exactly what I am saying," I said, frustrated. "Predictions are not always accurate. I'm not getting what you're aiming at. Why can't we peek into our future?"

"Ah! Don't you see the confusion and chaos that would enter our lives if we knew what was coming for certain? If we knew who would be elected the next president, what stock prices would be, who was going to be admitted to Harvard or Stamperd, and the exact date each of us will die . . ."

"I get it, Bill, I get it," I said. "All those scenarios are terrifying."

"You see? Human beings do best when left alone, free of knowledge of future events."

I smiled. "Well, you've said you're nothing more than a scientist, but now you just laid out a powerful philosophy!"

"Did I?" He looked bemused.

"You did!" I exclaimed. "You're a philosopher, Bill!"

After laughing with me, Bill pulled himself together. Looking directly at me, he said earnestly, "After all, Peonia, you did what you wanted to do, and that served as the grand purpose of my machine."

Moved, I reached up and placed a hand on his shoulder. "Thank you." Grinning, I continued. "And you, Bill, you broke free from the cocoon of a scientist and became a philosopher—and a great one!"

About the Author

Pejay Bradley was born in Seoul, Korea. She graduated from Seoul National University and later came to USA, became a lawyer, and practiced law in Florida. She currently lives in San Francisco Bay Area.

www.ingramcontent.com/pod-product-compliance
Lightning Source LLC
Chambersburg PA
CBHW030312060726
47498CB00002BB/594